HONOUR

Noah Beaton-Stokell

Honour

tellwell

Tellwell Talent
www.tellwell.ca

ISBN
978-0-2288-3290-4 (Hardcover)
978-0-2288-3291-1 (Paperback)
978-0-2288-3289-8 (eBook)

CHAPTER 1

~1590 - Ikebe Village~

"Lower, Kenji! How do you plan on becoming a samurai when you cannot even do proper push ups? You should be feeling your nose touch the grass beneath you!" Ichiro yelled down to his nephew Kenji.

"I'm going as low as I can Uncle. I'm only ten you know." Kenji huffed back at his uncle.

"You know, your father was doing push ups lower than you on nothing but his two little fingers when he was three." Ichiro retorted.

"You made that up!" Kenji laughed, losing his strength and collapsing to the grass.

"Oh no, I'm serious!" Ichiro replied, holding back a grin. "He could run from here to Sekigahara by the time he turned five!"

"No way!" Kenji said, lying on the grass looking up at his Uncle.

"Yes, my boy! And more than that, he could ev-"

Ichiro was cut off by a loud bang coming from over the hill.

"What was that, Uncle Ichiro?"

"I am not sure - perhaps some of the men are cutting down trees to make way for a race track for you."

"Uncle, you're lying again!" Kenji laughed.

"I am not!" Ichiro argued. "I heard them talking about it just last week!"

"Ichiro!" A woman cried out from the far side of the hill.

"Look, here comes your mother. We will have to tell her you did one hundred push ups this morning."

"Yes!" Kenji chuckled.

"Ichiro! Soldiers!" Yelled Maru, Kenji's mother, who was carrying a bag hung over her shoulder. "They bear the mark of Tokugawa!"

"Where?"

"By the northern gate! There's too many for our men to hold back!" Maru said in a panic.

"I will be right there! Kenji, you stay here with your mother."

Kenji's mother stilled. She looked into her brother's eyes. "No! You need to take him. He will be safer with you. Take him to the woods out toward the southern road."

"You know I cannot do that." Ichiro replied softly.

"You have to. It will be better for him. You will give him a chance," Maru pleaded.

"Fine. Kenji, up! We are going to go train in the woods." Ichiro commanded.

"What's going on Uncle?" Kenji asked, clearly worried about the exchange.

"There is no time son. Uncle Ichiro is going to take you to the woods now," Maru insisted, trying for a calming tone, her voice shaking.

"But why, mama?" Kenji asked, desperate for answers.

"I will explain later Kenji, but for now we must go to the woods." Ichiro replied.

"Here, take these. Supplies from the house. Your equipment should be in there too," Maru said, thrusting the bag into Ichiro's hands.

"I will keep him safe." Ichiro looked steadily into Maru's eyes.

Maru turned to hug Kenji. "I love you my boy. Stay close to your Uncle Ichiro, okay?"

"I will." Kenji replied, hugging his mother back.

Another loud noise from over the hill had Kenji release his mother, looking startled.

"Mama, who are they?" Kenji asked, looking toward the hill.

Panicked, she turned to look.

"Go, now! Both of you!" Maru ordered.

Behind his mother, Kenji could see orange rising from the crest of the hill. There were buildings on fire.

"Mama!"

...

Kenji sat up quickly, startling himself. His eyes were darting frantically, his breathing short and quick.

"Bad dream Kenji?" Ichiro asked while resting against a fallen log.

"Yes Uncle, always the same one. We are back in the village, the last time I saw my mother."

"That was nine years ago now Kenji."

"I know Uncle, but I still think about it. I cannot help it."

"You have to learn to let go of the past, my boy. It makes the future easier to approach."

"How am I supposed to do that when all we do is sit around and think? What else am I to think about?"

"How about your training? When was the last time you swung your swords?"

Ichiro glanced at the two swords hung on Kenji's back. One was a long samurai sword Kenji had taken from a bandit on the road, a few weeks back. It was sturdy enough, but needed constant attention to stay sharp. The second was a short samurai sword that originally belonged to Kenji's father. It had been in his family for generations, and had been in the pack his mother had given them nine years before. The hilt had a carving of a golden dragon wrapped around the base of the blade and the handle had red rope wound tightly around it to give the one holding it a better grip.

"I practice all the time. Besides, we haven't seen anyone in days. The roads are clear. There is nothing to do out here."

"There is always something to do. Never waste a moment Kenji, every moment can be used to accomplish something."

"What have we accomplished? We have been sitting here for two days so you can get strength back in that knee of yours. I could accomplish more without you."

Ichiro gazed up at Kenji with disappointment on his face.

With that, Kenji stood up.

"I am going to check the traps."

Kenji turned toward the woods and began to walk out toward the nearest traps, not daring to look back and meet the gaze of his uncle.

Kenji needed to clear his head. He was increasingly frustrated with stopping for his uncle to regain his strength. Could he accomplish more without him? No. He knew that was not true. He would not have survived a month without Ichiro's guidance. Kenji took a deep breath and looked up through the branches, trying to see if any rays of sun could find their way through the leaves. It was so dark in this forest. The leaves created a blanket over the woods, shielding everything underneath from the warmth of the sun.

There was a rustle behind him. Kenji pulled his right arm back to grasp the handle of his short sword and turned swiftly to meet the sound. Tightening his grip, Kenji steadied himself and prepared to meet whatever had created the noise.

A rabbit emerged from under a bush and met his gaze.

Kenji released the breath he was holding, let go of his sword and let his arm fall to his waist. Curious, the rabbit looked toward Kenji's hand, perhaps expecting something to be inside it.

"What are you looking at?" Kenji asked the rabbit.

Without a response the rabbit hopped past Kenji and into the hole of a nearby tree trunk.

'Look what you have become Kenji, talking to rabbits.'

Kenji chuckled to himself and bent down to fix a new trap at his feet hoping the rabbit may come back the same way.

Where should we go next? Probably continue north, he thought. There was a section of forest he and Ichiro had yet to travel. They had been staying south, always sure to stay away from the main path to avoid drawing attention. Kenji knew the land to the north was dangerous. The war was up north and Ichiro thought Sekigahara might be Tokugawa's next target. They needed to stay as far away from the fight as they could, at least for now. Kenji's thought was interrupted by a voice behind him.

"What do we have here? A wanderer who has lost his way? Get up." A voice said over Kenji's shoulder.

You were careless Kenji, too focused on a day dream, he thought. Kenji stood slowly, mentally noting how long it would take for his hand to reach his sword. Turning around to meet the voice, Kenji was met by four men, brandishing swords, clearly long untended.

"Nice swords you have there. Mind if I take 'em?" grinned the leader of the group.

Ignoring the initial question, Kenji looked over the men. The man questioning him was around his height, and had an aura of leadership about him. He wore a wooden breastplate with no marking, and leather shoulder pads that left his armpits vulnerable, but not much else on his upper half. The men behind him were nothing special, all dressed in light cloth and carrying satchels over their shoulders. They had clearly been on the road for days without much rest, evident by the bags under their eyes and the slump in their shoulders, probably by the command of the man who was so close to Kenji he could smell his breath.

"Hey! I asked you a question, boy!" The man shouted at Kenji.

Wiping the spit from his face, Kenji looked back at him with a level gaze.

"These swords aren't for sale. But if you want, I could show you how they work," Kenji said with mock seriousness.

"You've got some nerve on you boy. It seems we might need to teach you a lesson," the leader spit.

As if on cue, the men behind the leader started to form a semi circle in front of Kenji, noticeably tightening the grip on their swords.

"Believe me, it would be better if you all walked away." Kenji said calmly.

"Oh no. I'm not leaving until I get those shiny swords off your back," the man retorted.

Sighing, Kenji stepped his right foot back and dug his heel in behind him for support. Loosening his shoulders and surveying the gang in front of him, Kenji awaited the man's next move.

"If this is really how you want to play this..." Kenji replied.

"Let's get those swords boys." The man said with a half-cocked grin.

The man tensed and slightly lowered his shoulders, showing Kenji he needed to prepare for an overhead blow. The man did just that, and swung over the top of Kenji's head, wanting to quickly end the fight. Kenji reached back to grasp both of his swords, and unsheathed them, forming an 'x' over his head to meet the man's weapon. The swords collided with a clang of metal that rang through the trees, and Kenji twisted his back heel to keep his footing. Clearly unprepared for a successful response to his attack, the man stepped back and let out a cry while thrusting his sword at Kenji's midsection. Kenji moved to his left as if sliding across ice, and swung his left arm up underneath the man's armpit. His sword connected in the section where the wooden breast plate and his shoulder pad met. In one clean cut, the man's arm fell motionless to the grass. The leader let out a cry, and fell to the ground, out cold. Kenji pivoted to face the last three men, swiping down with his left arm in an attempt to remove some blood from the blade. The men looked down toward their leader, now lying in a pool of blood, his severed arm still grasping the handle of his sword. Two of the men readied themselves on either side of Kenji. The first attack came from Kenji's right, and the man swung sideways aiming for Kenji's rib cage. Kenji turned his sword up to block the incoming strike. At the same moment, the man to Kenji's left swung for the top of Kenji's head, the same as his fallen leader had done. Kenji blocked this as well bending his knees to hold his ground again both attacks. Having blocked the overhead swing to his left, Kenji gave a swift kick to the man's jaw, causing him to fall backwards to the grass. Now able to focus on the second attacker, Kenji parried the sword to the right and turned to face the man. Using the momentum of his turn, Kenji thrust his left sword straight through the attacker's abdomen. The man's body folded over the sword before collapsing to the ground alongside his former leader. A cry came from the final man who had yet to engage him. Kenji readied himself as the man charged for him. Watching the man as he got closer, Kenji side stepped to his right and gave a strong downward strike across the man's back, and he joined his companions on the grass. Straightening up, Kenji took a deep breath. It had been awhile since he was directly challenged.

Suddenly there was another noise behind him. Kenji pivoted to face it, readying his sword. Kenji was met with the gaping mouth of the man he had kicked moments before. The man stood motionless, sword above his head, mouth hanging open. Kenji looked down and saw a sword sticking out of the man's stomach, pointed toward him. The sword was pulled out and the man collapsed to the ground, revealing Ichiro, breathing heavy, standing behind him.

"What happened to not drawing attention to ourselves?" Ichiro asked, pulling out a cloth to clean his blade.

"They came to me, Uncle. I was not about to give up my swords." Kenji replied.

"So how exactly did they come to sneak up on you? You must always be aware of your surroundings. That was foolish and clumsy."

"I had it under control." Kenji shot back.

"Be that as it may, those were unnecessary deaths that could have been avoided."

"They were common bandits. The world is better off without them."

"I do not disagree with you, but they could have been driven off. There was no need to kill them."

Kenji sheathed his swords. His uncle was right.

"Now let us gather what we can from the bodies and head back to camp. It is nearly sundown."

Kenji followed his uncle's lead and started to grab the flasks full of water and the small rations of stale bread and nuts from the men's satchels. Not much else was needed from the corpses so Kenji and Ichiro began carrying the bodies to set them down in the bushes. Once the last of the men was placed in the undergrowth, Kenji and Ichiro walked back to camp without saying another word.

Sitting down near the fire, Kenji pulled out a cloth and began cleaning his swords as his uncle had shown him many times. The blood from the previous engagement was already beginning to crust on the blades but Kenji did not want to spare water to clean them, instead scrubbing until all the traces were gone. Ichiro was already asleep lying against the trunk of a tree, his breathing heavy; just killing the one man had taken a lot out of him, even if he would not admit it. Kenji placed his swords down to his sides. He could feel his eyes getting heavy, not wanting the burden of staying open. Kenji stood to snuff out the fire before lying back down. Kenji needed his strength, for tomorrow was another new day and he needed to be ready for whatever was ahead.

CHAPTER 2

~1599 - Orochi Forest~

Kenji awoke to feel the rising sun on his face. A handful of rays had found their way through the canopy above. Blinking twice to try and sharpen his vision, Kenji slowly stood and stretched his back. Ichiro was burying the remains of the coals clinging to the few remaining logs.

"We should take stock and move on from here." Ichiro said, without looking up from the ashes.

"Yes, Uncle." Kenji replied still drowsy.

Kenji bent to pick up and sheath his swords then moved to his pack to check what he had left. There was enough water for them to last at least another three days, and the rations picked up from the bandits ensured they could do the same food wise. Kenji took a drink from his bottle and took a deep breath in, enjoying how the water made his throat feel chilled and awake.

"So, it's north for us then Uncle?"

"Yes, I wanted to avoid it but I fear we do not have much of a choice. There is not much left in this part of the forest for us."

"Do you really think Tokugawa would try and take Sekigahara? That would be a bold move, even for him."

"I do. Sekigahara is a place of great importance, very strategic. If he conquers it, it could mean he would control Japan itself."

"But how can one man rule Japan? He doesn't have the manpower to maintain control."

"His armies have grown exponentially, but it is not all about manpower. Tokugawa is as great a strategist as he is ruthless. He gains the respect and fear of his followers and his enemies."

"Did you know him Uncle? You speak of him as if you did."

"Yes. I was a leader of a samurai legion, as you know, and Tokugawa was a captain within the same army. We collaborated on more than one occasion. The man is smart and tactical and uses strategies not often used by other generals to achieve his victories."

"So, you two were close?"

"I would not say that. We had to get along for the sake of our armies. We achieved great things together, but it was rare we saw eye to eye."

"Is that why he attacked Ikebe?"

"No, do not be foolish. Tokugawa is not one to linger over a personal vendetta. I am sure he knew I was there, but Ikebe was going to be in danger whether I was there or not."

"Would he know you now, if he saw you again?"

"I am sure he would, we spent a lot of time together on the battlefield. My face is not one he would easily forget."

"Then maybe we shouldn't go north, it could be too much of a risk."

"I am afraid we do not have much of a choice, Kenji. We are running out of options. We will stick to the treeline and stay out of sight of the patrols."

"We should get moving then."

"You are right; we have much ground to cover."

Ichiro stood slowly, bracing himself against the fallen log he was sitting on. His knee was weak; it was obvious to Kenji, but he knew it would not be wise to mention it. Deciding it best to ignore his uncle's pain, Kenji gathered up the remaining supplies and stored them in his satchel.

"Ready, Uncle?"

"Yes, it is time to go. I will follow you."

"Make sure you keep up, I don't want to have to carry you too."

Ichiro replied with a faint smile and followed Kenji through a clearing in the trees.

~1585 - Ikebe Village~

"Uncle Ichiro! Come get me!" Kenji waved his arms above his head, signalling for his uncle to chase after him.

"You better go; he has lots of energy to burn off." Maru said with a grin.

"Why is it always tag? Why can he not enjoy sitting and looking at the birds?" Ichiro replied slowly getting to his feet.

"He is just a child; you always played tag with me when we were younger."

"That was when I had two good knees. And you were not very fast."

"Do not get your knee kicked by a horse and you would not need to complain. And I was plenty fast."

"You seem to forget that horse was carrying a man who was not exactly looking to make friends with me."

"Uncle Ichiro!"

"I'm coming Kenji! If I collapse chasing him, I am blaming it on you."

"How can you say that?"

"Because you did not stop me from joining the army."

Ichiro turned and jogged after Kenji.

"I would not have been able to stop you if I tried," Maru called after her brother.

~1599 - The edge of Orochi Forest~

"Uncle, look, footprints." Kenji knelt down to examine the boot marks in the mud.

"The steps are side by side, walking in unison. It must have been a patrol." Ichiro said, leaning over Kenji's shoulder.

"They're still fresh, they must have just passed. We should be careful."

"Kenji, get down!" Ichiro hissed.

Kenji crouched down and readied his sword.

"What is it, Uncle?"

"Look, there at the edge of the treeline."

Ichiro was right. At the edge of the forest walked eight men. Soldiers each equipped with standard armour and swords, moving toward the field outside the forest. Their eyes were alert, constantly darting around, perhaps expecting something to happen.

"They must be from Sekigahara. We are too close to the city." Ichiro stood, trying to look for signs of the city on the horizon.

Suddenly, one soldier in the back of the group yelled out. His knees collapsed and his body went limp as he fell to the ground. The man beside him knelt down and removed an arrow from his neck.

"Ambush!"

The soldiers drew their swords and formed a circle around their deceased partner.

"There, look! Cavalry!"

Soldiers on horseback charged from the horizon, spears pointed toward the circle of men. The panicked patrol turned to face the advancing attack but the horses had already gotten too close. The lead horseman ran through the patrol, his spear piercing a soldier and carrying him a short way before letting him fall from his spear. Within moments, the patrol was surrounded by horsemen all jabbing down at them with their weapons.

"I should go help them." Kenji reached for his sword.

"No, Kenji. It is too late for them now."

Ichiro was right. When Kenji looked back the men had disappeared behind a crowd of horses. The only sound was of the horses and the sheathing of the horsemen's weapons.

"I could have helped them."

"Kenji, do not be rash, the men were dead when they left the city. We have no reason to put ourselves in danger."

"Uncle..."

Ichiro breathed out slowly, feeling the steel of a sword touch his neck.

"Turn slowly." A voice from behind Ichiro commanded.

Ichiro did as instructed, and came face to face with a soldier who bore the mark of Tokugawa on his breastplate. Kenji reached for his sword but was stopped by the tip of an arrow that was mere inches from his face. They had been surrounded.

"This is brilliant." Kenji exclaimed. "I'm blaming this one on you."

"How so, nephew?"

"You were supposed to be watching our backs, that's why you were behind."

"I was not the one staring at mud."

"I was..."

"Quiet!" A soldier yelled back to them. "Get moving!"

Kenji and Ichiro were being led by four soldiers toward the hill from where the horsemen charged. Kenji looked out at the serene and fields as they passed. The grass was flowing in unison with the wind and the birds were flying above, not bothered by the actions on the ground. *Could this really turn into a battleground?* Kenji thought. He hoped not.

The peaceful image of the valley was washed away when the men led them over the crest of the hill. Kenji's mouth involuntarily fell open as he looked out across the countless rows of tents that lined the opposite side of the hill. Crude barricades were set up, lining the outside of the camp, which was so big it may as well have been a military compound. Flags bearing the mark of Tokugawa waved above the tents, and soldiers rushed from in and around the spaces in between.

Kenji and Ichiro were moved to a tent that looked identical to the thousands around them.

"Wait in here." One of the soldiers said. "There's someone who will want to meet with you."

The guard left without another word and Kenji and Ichiro were left to wait alone. Their weapons were confiscated, but to their surprise, their hands remained unbound.

Ichiro knelt down on a floor mat in the centre of the tent and closed his eyes.

"What's the plan Uncle? It looks like only two guards were left outside."

"Patience Kenji. Remember this is not our fight. We will explain ourselves and they will let us go."

"You really believe that?"

"I do. They have no reason to keep us here."

"Surely they cannot be reasoned with. The man who's coming to meet us, you think it could be him?"

"Perhaps."

"You know if he's here, you will not be able to charm your way out if this one, Uncle. The way you described it, you two didn't exactly part as friends."

"Yet we are not enemies. As I said, he has no reason to keep us here. He is too focused on his war to be bothered with us."

"Listen, footsteps."

Ichiro looked toward the entrance flap of the tent but did not get up from the mat, he simply waited to see who would enter to join them.

A hand came through the tent and pushed the flap to the side revealing a large man clad in heavy armour. His size made him almost unable to stand straight within the confines of the tent. He looked middle aged yet that did not distract from how imposing he was – and how easily he could likely win in a test of strength. Kenji glanced toward Ichiro, silently asking the obvious question. Was that Tokugawa?

The man spoke in a lumbering but calm voice.

"Ichiro. You are the last person I expected to see this morning, even less so in our camp."

"Tensu, still under the boot of Tokugawa I see?"

"I follow the rightful ruler of Japan. Lord Tokugawa will rule Japan."

"I have no interest in your war. We just wish to have our things returned to us and we will be on our way."

Tensu seemed unbothered by Ichiro's response, now focused fully on Kenji.

"Who is this you have with you? I do not remember you having a son."

Ichiro stood now to answer Tensu's new question.

"No, not my son, but he is family."

"Brother then? He looks too young for that. A nephew perhaps?"

Ichiro did not respond, which gave Tensu the answer he sought.

"Where is he? Is he here with you, or cowering behind his fortress?" Ichiro asked, moving a step closer toward Tensu.

"Lord Tokugawa does not cower. You should mind your tongue."

Ichiro smiled, pleased to have touched a nerve.

"So, he is here then?"

"Yes. He is here. He will most definitely want to see you as well. You two have a lot to catch up on."

"As he said, we have no interest in this war. We just want our supplies back and we'll leave." Kenji piped up from his place at the back corner of the tent.

"You may have your things back in due time. First however, you must freshen up for your meeting with Lord Tokugawa. I will arrange a meeting in the evening."

"That is so very kind of you. What a mannered soldier you have become, Tensu." Ichiro ushered him toward the entrance, indicating an end to the conversation.

"Hmph." Tensu turned and left the tent, closing the flap behind him.

"Another friend of yours, Uncle?"

"That was Tensu. He was a soldier under my command, but he always made it clear he preferred Tokugawa's leadership over mine."

A young woman entered with a tray of food and drink, followed by another woman carrying a bowl of warm water and cloths, and a bundle of fresh clothes.

Ichiro ignored their entrance and continued on.

"Tensu is a skilled fighter but was always too quick to come to decisions. Very reckless. It is only by luck he has not been killed in this war yet."

The women left the offerings and retreated from the tent as quickly as they had entered.

"So, he's Tokugawa's second?"

"It would seem so, yes. It must be why he was chosen to come see us."

"And we're going to accept?"

"We do not have another choice right now Kenji. When we meet with him, let me do the talking. And only speak when being addressed directly."

"Well, we better get ready; it seems we have a dinner date with your old friend."

Kenji began to remove his shirt, walking toward the bowl of warm water.

"What do you think he'll want from us?" Kenji asked beginning to wring out a cloth.

"I am not sure. Knowing him, it will be some sort of favour."

"And we'll grant him his favour?"

"Yes, if it means our freedom we will."

"I don't care for this Uncle." Kenji had washed his upper half and had begun putting one of the new shirts on.

"I do not like it any more than you do Kenji, but our hands are tied here."

"On the bright side, this food looks more edible than what we've been surviving off of."

Kenji sat down to begin eating some of the vegetables from the tray, not noticing how fast he was consuming it. Ichiro joined him, taking a pair of chopsticks and reaching for a bowl of rice.

"I cannot argue there." Ichiro replied.

Kenji and Ichiro sat in silence, consuming more food than either of them had seen in months.

CHAPTER 3

Two hours passed before a woman walked into the tent to summon Kenji and Ichiro.

"Follow me please." The woman said, gesturing to the entrance.

They stood and followed the woman outside. The sun was setting, and Kenji could see the last bit peeking over the crest of the hill. Every tent was filled with soldiers winding down for the evening, drinking and reminiscing. Some were lying down for the night, while others were getting dressed, preparing to relieve their fellow soldiers for the night watch. Kenji followed Ichiro and the woman to a large tent at the back of the camp. It stood out from the rest, with a grand entrance marked by flags and adorned with decorations. A white canvas hung over the entrance and underneath it stood two daunting men. Completely still, the men stared, equipped with heavy steel armour, decorated with symbols surrounding Tokugawa's crest. They had long curved swords hanging from their waists with one hand resting on the hilts. *Samurai*, Kenji thought to himself.

Kenji stepped through the entrance flap after the woman and his uncle, and was taken aback by the size of the interior. It was bigger than some houses in his old village. To either side of the entrance stood two more men, near identical to the two outside. Directly ahead was a large open space with a straw mat covering most of the ground area. There were three extensions to this tent - one directly in front of him, which he could see had a desk in the centre, and two more off to the sides, their contents out of view. The woman led them to the room at the back with the desk in its centre. Another two samurai stood behind the desk guarding an additional flap leading further into the tent.

"Please wait here. Lord Tokugawa will be with you shortly," the woman said with a slight bow, and left the room.

"Am I standing straight enough Uncle?" Kenji asked with a grin.

"Quiet, this is not the time. Remember - let me talk to him."

"Should I curtsey for him?"

"Kenji."

"Fine."

The flap opened and Tensu entered the room.

"You will kneel before the rightful ruler of Japan, Lord Tokugawa."

The samurai dropped their hands to their sides standing at attention without command. Ichiro knelt down and Kenji followed suit.

Tensu held open the flap and he entered. Black steel plate armour edged with gold trim covered the man who had immediate control over the room. He sat, not yet speaking, and folded his hands on top of his desk.

"You may stand." Tensu commanded.

Ichiro stood and placed his hands behind his back. Kenji did the same.

"My Lord Tokugawa, I come before you, humbled by your presence, asking for the return of our weapons, and for safe passage back into the woods. There we will remain out of your way."

Kenji was shocked. Never had he seen his uncle overpowered like this. Never had Ichiro shown himself to be inferior to another man, not to mention a man who had yet to say a single word.

"My Lord Tokugawa, we found them outside of our camp, on the edge of Orochi forest."

Tokugawa acknowledged Tensu but stared now directly at Kenji. His eyes drilled into him. Kenji felt as if Tokugawa could stare right through him, learning everything about him. Kenji straightened his posture. Ichiro spoke again.

"Lord Tokugawa, what say you to our request?"

"Who is the boy?" Tokugawa asked with such intent his question now became top priority.

"He is his family sir, tha-"

Tokugawa's hand went up and Tensu was silenced.

"I asked Ichiro."

Tensu took a step back, his posture lowered.

"Ichiro you do not have a son, so who is the boy?" Tokugawa asked again.

"He is my nephew. I have raised him for most of his life."

"Very well." Tokugawa accepted the answer but did not seem satisfied.

Kenji shuffled nervously from his place beside Ichiro.

"I have a task for you." Tokugawa was again staring directly at Kenji. "Complete it and you shall be granted your weapons and safe passage."

"Uh yes, what is it my Lord?" Kenji felt sour calling this man his lord.

"Have you ever killed a man?"

"I have sir, yes."

"Would you do it again to secure your freedom?"

"Wait." Ichiro intervened. "You cannot just have hi-"

Again Tokugawa's hand raised and Ichiro this time was silenced. Kenji tried to hide his surprise seeing his strong uncle put in his place.

"Who is my target my Lord?" Kenji asked.

Tokugawa stood up and the room of men took a step back. As Tokugawa moved to admire a bonsai in the corner of the room, he spoke again.

"As you are no doubt aware, I am at war and my next target is the city of Sekigahara. When we win, I will become sole ruler of Japan - however, their forces admittedly outnumber my own. There is a man orchestrating the rebellion against me. I need him eliminated."

"Just give me the name my Lord." Kenji tried to sound as confident as he could manage.

"I need you to kill Ishiru Mitsunari," Tokugawa said, still gazing at the bonsai.

"My Lord, you want me to kill the leader of the Western Army? His home is in Sekigahara, is it not?"

"You are correct, that is why I cannot get to him myself. But you are one man, a man who could slip in unnoticed."

Tokugawa turned to face Kenji again.

"This is not a question. You will kill Mitsunari and return to me his family crest, which he keeps on his person at all times. Only then will you receive your supplies and safe passage. is all."

Kenji and Ichiro bowed respectfully to Tokugawa but he had already made his leave through the flap of the tent. Tensu stepped forward.

"You will complete the task tomorrow night. You may spend your time until then within this camp, and see the quartermaster tomorrow morning to receive the tools you will need."

Kenji bowed to Tensu and received a bow in return. This time it was Ichiro who had already left.

CHAPTER 4

Kenji left the command tent with an uneasy feeling in his stomach. Ichiro had trained him well, but this was a different task altogether. Assassinating someone? This was not what Ichiro trained him to do. Kenji sat outside of the tent, contemplating how he would do it. Killing someone in battle was not the hard part, but assassinating a person was difficult. There was no honour in it. Kenji could hear his uncle's voice in his head, "Kenji, to kill someone has its consequences, you know this. But if you must take a life, you must face them openly, give them an honourable death. To kill a person without honour is to dishonour yourself." Suddenly Kenji felt a pain in his rib, he had been kicked by a passing soldier.

"Get up! Out of the way!" A soldier was yelling down to Kenji.

He realized he was sitting in the middle of the path. Kenji stood up and looked back at the man.

"Did you not hear me boy? Get out of the way!"

It took every ounce of self control Kenji had to not drop the man where he stood. Instead Kenji took a breath.

"My apologies, I'll take my leave."

Kenji turned his back to the man and made his way back to the tent where he hoped Ichiro was waiting. He could hear the men behind him laughing about something but continued to walk away, unclenching his fist.

When Kenji arrived back at the tent, he was worried to see Ichiro was not there. "*Where did you go, old man?*" Kenji closed the tent flap, it was late now. The sun had hidden behind the horizon, shrouding the unlit camp in darkness. Lighting a candle, Kenji washed his face with what water remained in the bowl. He looked down, noticing his own reflection in the bottom of the bowl, barely recognizing the face stared back at him. His dark brown hair was short but somehow still messy and his eyes were tired, with bags under them. Some dirt still remained on his skin even with the water he used. They had been on the road for a long time.

"Man, I need to shave." Kenji said to himself. He rubbed his hand across the stubble that had formed on his jaw. "Ah, in the morning."

Kenji removed his clothes and left them by the side of the bed. The bed was not much but, better than the ground he was used to, covered in grass if he was lucky. Laying down, Kenji rolled over toward the candle and within a short breath he was again shrouded in darkness.

~1587 - Ikebe Village~

"Whoa Uncle, it's heavy!"

"It may feel like that now Kenji, but with time and training it will begin to feel like an extension of your arm."

Kenji gripped the wooden training sword with both hands and raised it up over his head.

"Uncle, look at me!"

"Yes, Kenji that is very impressive, but remember why I am teaching you. This is not a game."

"I know." Kenji lowered the sword again.

"Now let us start."

Ichiro stood beside Kenji with a wooden sword of his own.

"Raise your sword up my boy, mirror my actions."

Kenji followed along raising his training sword so the hilt was chest height.

"Now follow along. Raise the sword up so the handle is over your shoulder then strike down. Think of coming across your body, ending by pointing the blade toward the grass."

Ichiro swept the sword across his body. Kenji tried copying his uncle, but lost his balance on the swing. The sword was heavier than he was ready for.

"Make sure to plant your feet. Staying stable is very important is you want a powerful strike. Try again."

Kenji repositioned his feet, one in front of the other. Raising the sword up he took another swing this time able to steady himself with his feet.

"There, that is better. Now do it again."

Kenji took swing after swing, each time striking slightly harder and slightly faster.

"Look Uncle Ichiro, I didn't fall!"

"That is right, you are getting the hang of it."

"Uncle?"

"Yes, Kenji?"

"Are you showing me this so I can fight with you when you go away again?"

"Kenji I am not going away again. This time I am here to stay, there is no more fighting for me."

"So why are we doing this then Uncle?"

"So that if you ever need to defend yourself, you will be prepared."

"Will I have to kill someone? Like you have?"

Ichiro sighed and put his hand on Kenji's shoulder.

"Kenji, I want you to listen to what I have to say very carefully. To kill someone has its consequences. But if you must take a person's life you must face them openly, give them an honourable death. To kill a person without honour is to dishonour yourself.

Do you understand? You do not take another life unless it is absolutely necessary."

"I understand."

"Good, now get back to your strikes, we have a lot to cover today."

~1599 - Tokugawa's Camp~

Kenji woke this time of his own choice. He had not slept that well in as long as he could remember. For awhile he just laid there, not wanting to leave the warmth and comfort of the bed. But with some regret he got up, and walked over to put his clothes back on. Kenji walked out of the tent and was surprised to see the sun sitting high above the camp. How long had he slept? The camp was as busy as it was yesterday. Soldiers talking, equipment being carried back and forth, and men always standing watch on the borders.

"Well, I have a whole day to waste. I cannot go until sundown anyway." Kenji said aloud.

Kenji went off in search of the quartermaster Tensu told him to find. The camp was a maze, tents as far as he could see blocking any sign of the horizon. It did not help that every tent looked the same. He knew where Tokugawa's tent was, so he made his way in that direction, hoping the quartermaster would be somewhere along his route. Along the way, Kenji heard a commotion behind one of the tents. His curiosity got the better of him and he decided to follow the noise.

When Kenji walked around the corner of a nearby tent, he saw a large group of soldiers standing in a circle all shouting and waving their arms in the air. Kenji tapped one of the soldiers on the arm.

"What's going on here?"

The soldier turned around and surprised Kenji. The soldier did not look much older than he was. His eyes were sharp, hiding the boy behind them. He smiled at Kenji and replied.

"Two of the soldiers are fighting, we place bets on who will win. It's a good way to wind down and for some of the men to let off steam."

Sure enough, when Kenji craned his neck to see past the crowd, two soldiers were inside a ring of men. Both men were sweating and breathing hard, trading punches and trying to keep their balance. It had been a long fight already it seemed.

"This is common?" Kenji asked.

"Oh yes. Usually there will be a couple of fights in a row."

"I see."

"Hey, I don't recognize you. You're not part of the army, right? You're the new guy the men talk about."

"I guess I am, yes."

"I'm Maku, nice to meet you." The boy stuck out his hand.

Kenji replied with a firm shake. Maku had a tighter grip than he was expecting.

"How did you end up in the army," Kenji asked, "you don't look all that old."

"I'm eighteen, and perfectly capable of serving my lord."

"I meant no offence."

"It's alright, I get that a lot. In truth I didn't choose this. My parents told me I had to for the betterment of Japan. Between you and me, I would much prefer to help my father with our rice paddy."

"I see. I suppose had my life gone differently I would be in your position as well."

"So why are you here if you're not in the army?"

A cheer erupted from the crowd behind Maku, interrupting Kenji's reply.

"Looks like someone won."

Maku looked back to try to identify the winner. Kenji followed his glance. There was one man lying on the ground clutching his chest, the other man casting a shadow over him basking in the glory the win had given him. A man beside Kenji bumped him.

"Hey, you're the new kid who came in with the old man, right?"

"Yes, what's it to you?"

"I heard Lord Tokugawa is giving you a special assignment, but you don't look so tough to me."

"Looks can be deceiving." Kenji turned to walk away. The man grabbed his shoulder.

"If you're so tough why don't you prove it?"

The back end of the crowd had now shifted their attention to the man threatening Kenji.

"Sorry, but I have somewhere to be."

"Don't worry, I'll beat you so quick you'll have plenty of time to get where you're going."

The crowd laughed in support of the soldier.

"Look, I don't have time." Kenji was starting to get impatient.

"Nonsense, one quick round. You win, I'll buy you a drink. But if I win you have to tell Lord Tokugawa I'll take on the assignment."

Maku looked anxiously toward Kenji for his response. Kenji walked toward the centre of the crowd removing his shirt.

"Let's get this over with."

A small cheer was let out from the crowd of soldiers and voices could be heard placing down quick bets.

Kenji stretched his neck as the other man joined him in the ring. The man was taller and broader than Kenji but much more cocky - he would use it against him. The man removed his breast plate and shirt and began pumping up the crowd in his favour. Something caught Kenji's eye. He looked up past the crowd. A small wooden platform had been constructed and Tensu was standing on top of it, and below him seated at the table was Tokugawa. Arms folded, Tokugawa leaned against the table top and looked directly at Kenji.

"Are you ready boy? I hope you're prepared to lose your special mission."

Kenji lifted his fists to his chin and put one foot in front of the other. The man was large and likely used his weight to strike hard, which meant a hard, slow landing. Kenji knew this and shifted his weight to his front foot - he would need to move quickly.

The man swung first; a right hook aimed at Kenji's head. Kenji stepped left, ducking under the swing and with his right leg landed a side kick to the back of the man's knee. The man dropped to his knee but recovered quickly, turning to face Kenji again. He let out a yell and dove for Kenji's legs.

Wrapping his arms around him, the man stood and drove Kenji into the ground. Kenji exhaled sharply as his back hit the hard dirt. The man used his advantage and hit Kenji's chin hard with a left punch. Dazed, Kenji wrapped his legs around the man and pulled him down, covering his face against the man's chest. The man took another swing with his left arm but this one grazed the back of Kenji's head. Kenji laid back and drove his knee up underneath the man's chin. Now with the man dazed, Kenji grabbed hold of his left arm and held it out to the side, leaving room to swing his right leg over the man's neck. The man squirmed frantically as Kenji wrapped his left leg over his right shin closing around the man's neck. The man was furious now but also panicked. He tried to use his strength and drive Kenji back, even getting to his feet. Kenji arched his back to brace his shoulders against the ground and brought the man's left arm over to the other side, tightening this hold further.

"I've won, you should tap," Kenji said between breaths.

The man was not looking to lose - he fought hard, trying to buck Kenji's leg from his neck. But all he was doing was exhausting himself. Kenji reached up for the man's head and pulled it closer to him.

"You should tap," Kenji warned.

The man continued to fight but was starting to slow. Kenji pulled hard on his head and squeezed his legs together. After a couple of seconds and last attempt punches, the man stopped. His body went limp and he collapsed to the ground as Kenji released his hold. There was silence as Kenji stood, the crowd not daring to say a word. Maku emerged from the circle and knelt beside the man. He reached down to touch the man's neck.

"He's alive, just knocked out." Maku announced.

The crowd erupted in cheers. Soldiers came to applaud Kenji and give their respect. Kenji was not bothered by them. He was looking to the platform where Tokugawa looked down at him. His face bore the same expression only now he was leaning back in his chair.

"That was crazy!"

Maku had appeared beside Kenji once again and gave him a pat on the back.

"You've caused quite a stir around here. I bet you'll be the topic of conversation tonight."

"It was a waste of time. I have to go see someone."

"If you ever need anything while you're here just give me a shout. It would be an honour, Kenji."

Kenji began to walk away but turned back.

"Actually, I could use your help. I need to find the quartermaster before sundown. I was told to get some supplies from him."

"I can help with that. Follow me."

Maku was eager, and Kenji followed the energetic soldier.

"Where did you learn to do that?" Maku asked.

"I had a good teacher."

"Was it the old man you were brought here with?"

"Yes, it was."

Kenji was not looking for conversation but realized that was the price that came with Maku's directions.

"And you said you weren't a soldier?" Maku continued.

"No, I'm not. The man I came here with was though."

"Why don't you join, you'd have better odds than I do."

"It's not my fight."

"With respect Kenji, it's Japan's fight. This war will determine Japan's fate."

"Japan's fate will be decided with or without me."

"So, what were you doing before you were brought here then?"

Kenji ignored this question as they were approaching a large tent with a canvas extending out above them covering a wooden stand.

"Is this it?"

"Yes, here it is. The quartermaster is usually inside. Just knock on the top of the counter."

"Thank you Maku." Kenji extended his hand. Maku shook his hand and bowed to Kenji.

"My pleasure. Remember if you need anything else just come ask for me," Maku said and turned to leave. Kenji had himself a fan. *Well, it's better than an enemy,* he thought. Kenji approached the counter and knocked on the top, as Maku had instructed. There were rummaging sounds coming from the back of the tent, and within moments an elderly man appeared. Much older than Ichiro, Kenji could not help but wonder how the man was standing on his own.

"You must be the man Tensu spoke of," the man said, pointed a crooked finger at Kenji.

"That's right. I was told you would have equipment for me?"

"I do. Right this way please, and don't fall behind."

That would not be a problem. The man took four steps before Kenji needed to take one. As they walked toward the back of the tent Kenji eyed the room. There were hundreds of swords, bows and pikes lining the walls, and boxes covered the ground. The size of the tent was misleading from the outside.

"Right over here." The man led Kenji to an open crate.

"These are what I was told to supply you with for your assignment."

Inside the box were folded clothes, black with grey lining, and a pair of black shoes. They were stacked on top of other obscured objects in the box.

"What's underneath?" Kenji asked, not able to quell his curiosity.

"Well, you have a knife, nothing special, but still effective at stabbing should the need arise. Some rope, which should help with the wall, and these." The man smiled as he pulled a smaller box out from under the clothes.

"I was told to prepare these special for you." The man seemed very pleased with himself as he opened the small box.

"What are they?" Kenji stared down at the small metal tube and the two metal spheres that lay inside the box.

"This is the most important item," the man said as he held up the tube. "This is what will get the job done. Slip a drop of this into Mitsunari's drink, or right into his mouth if you'd like, and the liquid will do the rest."

"So, it's a type of poison?"

"Precisely. Now these you must be very careful with. I have yet to use them myself or give them out to any of the soldiers. But Tokugawa thought they might come in handy."

"And what exactly are these?" Kenji picked up and examined one of the metal spheres.

"A new creation. If the outer casing is smashed, it will release a thick cloud of smoke, obscuring you from the vision of others."

"A quick escape route. Will they work?"

"Probably," the man replied, searching through another crate.

Great, I love doing things that will probably work, Kenji thought.

"If you're worried about them working, may I suggest not getting caught?"

"Oh thanks, I never thought of that," Kenji bit back sarcastically.

The man smiled and Kenji smiled back. He could not help himself.

"You should get ready, only a couple of hours until sundown. And you should check out the mess hall, good to get some energy before you leave." The man began to pack everything back inside the box.

"I will, thank you." Kenji took the packed box from the old man and left the tent.

"Good luck!" Kenji heard the man call out from his tent.

Kenji walked back to his tent and placed the box by the side of the bed. He knelt down beside the box and closed his eyes. *You need to do this. This is the only way out. To get safety for you and Ichiro.* He told himself. Suddenly his eyes opened. Where was Ichiro? He had not seen his uncle since yesterday. But Kenji knew he could not focus on that now. He needed to keep his mind on the task at hand. Ichiro was safe; there was no way for him to get out of the camp without a guard noticing. Kenji opened the box and removed the clothes. They were light and stretchy. Putting them on they felt tight, compressed to his body, but easy to move in. The shoes were almost sticky on the bottom, feeling like they were gripping the mat he was standing on. Next, he took out the rope and hung it in a loop around one shoulder. Finally, he grabbed the knife and holstered it to the belt wrapped around the waist of the shirt. He examined the second, smaller box and realized the smoke canisters and tube were lying on a small satchel, also made from black cloth. He put both smoke spheres and the tube filled with poison inside and hung it over his shoulder. As he was adjusting the fit of the satchel, a soldier came into the tent.

"Are you ready? It's nearly sundown."

"Yes, I'll be right out."

"Very good." The man left but was clearly waiting outside the flap for him.

I guess it's time to go, Kenji said to himself. Walking outside, Kenji was surprised at how fast the sun had begun to drop, painting the sky pink and orange.

"I've been instructed to take you to the castle walls and wait for your return by the treeline there."

"Very well. Lead on." Kenji tried to muster the most commanding voice he could.

"Right this way." The man took off at a jogging pace forcing Kenji to keep up with him. The two of them jogged past the border of the camp and up over the hill. Kenji looked back wondering which tent Ichiro could be in. *Unimportant,* he told himself again.

With the cover of darkness, they reached the treeline outside the wall. The wall was higher than Kenji had thought it would be. Towering over them, in the daytime it must overshadow the valley below it.

"Now remember, you have to kill Mitsunari before returning to me here, and if anyone gets between you and your goal, dispatch them as well."

Kenji nodded.

"Good luck, I'll be waiting here.

Kenji turned to the wall, surveying the top to look for any sentries that might be posted. Seeing no sign of lookouts, Kenji kept low and made his way to the wall. Pressing his back against it, he started to uncoil his rope then stopped. The wall behind him felt uneven. The wall had been constructed in such a way that every second brick was protruding out slightly from the one beside it. He could free climb it. Coiling the rope back up,

Kenji turned toward the wall. Checking his gear to make sure everything was secure, he lifted an arm up and grabbed hold of the highest brick he could reach. Anchoring his other foot to a lower brick he pulled himself up off the ground. Making sure to keep his limbs as straight as possible to avoid strain Kenji continued to climb, periodically changing the lead hand, to conserve as much energy as he could. Kenji could see the top - he was close now. Reaching his hand up again he pulled himself closer but quickly leaned in close when he heard a voice above him.

"So, you think we have enough men to hold the city?"

"What are you saying? Of course, we do."

"But what if Tokugawa does attack us here? The men have been saying he could attack any day now."

"Our scouts haven't seen any sign of him; if he attacks, we'll see it coming."

"I hope you're right."

The two soldiers walked on, not stopping to look down, to Kenji's fortune. His arms were straining, so he pulled himself up on top of the wall and sat with his legs hanging off the edge. The soldiers were out of earshot now. Kenji took a breath and scanned the ground for where his escort would be. He spotted him crouched behind a tree looking up at him. The man gave a wave and Kenji saluted him as he went out of his sight.

CHAPTER 5

Kenji turned to the city sprawled below him. Rooftops practically touching one another covered the streets. Kenji could use that, the less he touched the ground the better. The city seemed quiet, with only pockets of soldiers walking the streets and small detachments manning the wall. He spotted what he thought to be Mitsunari's house in the distance. It was two stories higher than the buildings around it and was at the other end of the city from where he was located on the wall. He could not make out enough of the house's details to plan a good route in, he would need to get closer. Kenji heard the distant sound of the soldiers, they were returning. Kenji took one step back then leapt to the nearest roof. The wall was higher than the rooftop so Kenji could land feet first. Stabilizing himself, he laid down and hugged the shingles as the men approached.

"I'm about done for the night, time to get some shut eye."

"I wish. I'm on duty for another hour still."

"Ah, sounds like fun."

"Shut up." The man jokingly punched his friend in the shoulder as they continued past.

Kenji got up on his knees, planning his route ahead. He ran across the rooftop and chose another to jump to. Making sure to mask his steps as much as he could, he moved from rooftop to rooftop all the while glancing to the sides hoping he was not seen. Kenji stopped as he got to a break in the buildings.

Mitsunari's house was on the other side of a courtyard now. Too far to jump. He would need to go to ground level. Kenji looked down toward the courtyard trying to find an opening in the guards' patrol patterns. Two men stood by the door at all times so that was not an option. One man on each side of the building walked back and forth, never straying from their route. Kenji spotted a small wall on the left side of the building he should be able to hide behind if he could get there. Kenji lowered himself down from the roof, bending his knees to absorb the impact. Making sure to stay crouched, Kenji peered around the corner trying to spot the patrolman he would have to get past.

"What was that?" A soldier sounded concerned and started to walk toward Kenji.

Kenji pinned his back to the wall and controlled his breathing. Making sure to stay calm, he lowered the sound of his breathing and stood still. The soldier walked to the corner of the building, inspecting where the sound came from. One more step from him and Kenji would be found out. He could smell him.

"Huh, must have been my imagination. I need rest."

Kenji let out a silent sigh and loosened his posture. Peering again around the corner he saw the soldier he needed to evade was walking with his back turned to him. Now was his chance. Kenji darted out from behind the corner and made a break for the small wall. Pinning his back to it again, Kenji stood still, waiting to see if the guards heard anything. It seemed they did not. Kenji took a step back from the wall and looked up, trying to find a way in. He could not stand here for long. There was a balcony three stories up from where he was. Mitsunari most likely had his quarters on the fifth and highest floor. This would have to do. He took out the rope from his satchel and unwound it. There was a metal hook on one end he was hoping he could snag on the railing. Checking to make sure he had still gone unnoticed, Kenji began to spin the rope. With momentum on his side he launched the rope up toward the balcony railing.

With a clang it bounced off the railing and fell back down to Kenji. Kenji dropped to a crouch waiting for a reaction from the guards. They did not seem to acknowledge it. He had been lucky so far but he could not afford to miss again. After waiting a moment, Kenji stood and tried again, launching the rope toward the railing for a second time. This time the hook caught on the low beam of the railing. Kenji gave it a tug to test the sturdiness.

This will have to do, Kenji told himself.

Grasping the rope with both hands, Kenji jumped and planted both feet on the wall. He wrapped the rope around one of his wrists and held tight with the other. With a deep breath, he began to ascend the wall. Taking his time, he moved one foot after the other while trying not to put much strain on the rope. He approached a lit room from the side. He flattened himself beside the window when he heard voices inside the room. The voices inside were too muffled to make out. Kenji continued on, being sure to go slowly past the windows. The balcony was almost within reach, but his arms were beginning to tire. He only had a few more steps to go. Suddenly he heard a crack and he stopped.

I really hope that's not the board he thought. The board was splintering. Kenji needed to move. He quickened his pace and kept one hand ready to reach for the railing. The cracking was getting louder. Kenji started to breathe faster as he got closer to the balcony railing. Another crack from the railing and Kenji was lowered down farther. He could feel the wood losing its strength. Kenji planted his feet and bent his knees. With a big pull on the rope Kenji leapt up and reached out for the balcony. The boards falling past him Kenji extended his arm and grabbed hold of the balcony platform. Hanging by his right arm Kenji looked down at the boards falling with the rope still attached.

Well, they'll notice that, he despaired to himself.

Kenji brought his left arm to the platform and hoisted himself up. Breathing heavily, he knelt beside the door.

Come on Kenji, that was nothing, he tried to reassure himself.

He got to his feet and slid open the door. The hallway was dark, and Kenji squinted to get a grasp on his surroundings. He was able to make out the outline of a hallway, and began moving along the wall looking for a staircase. He still had two more floors to ascend. The building was disturbingly quiet. Kenji tried to mask his footsteps as best as he could. Keeping to the wall he moved at a slow pace until he came to a staircase. He climbed the steps, being careful to look above him before he continued to move. Making it to the fourth floor, he stuck close to the wall.

A door opened in front of him and Kenji froze. A soldier walked out staggering and tightening his pants. Kenji plastered himself to the wall, holding his breath. The man looked up, his eyes not focused on any single point. As the man clambered toward Kenji, he tried to be still, hoping the dark hallway and his black clothing would camouflage him. The man walked slowly, each step barely holding him up. As the man got closer Kenji could smell the odour of alcohol. He came within inches of him. Within moments the man waddled past him, and Kenji released a long silent breath.

Kenji made his way to the room the man had emerged from, the door still open. He peeked around the doorway. There were two hanging lanterns lighting the centre of the room but leaving the corners obscured in darkness. Empty bottles were strewn on the floor - some were half full, most were empty. There was not much else in the room aside from a single bed with a night stand. On the bed lay two girls who looked Kenji's age. They were under the sheets asleep, their bodies intertwined. Kenji pulled the door to the room shut, leaving the girls to their sleep.

Moving on, Kenji found another set of stairs and ascended without seeing anyone. He was now on the top floor. This hallway was laid out differently. As Kenji got to the top of the stairs the hallway in front of him only extended forward with the rooms branching out from the sides of it. Kenji inched his way along the hallway making sure to step from heel to toe trying to keep his movement silent. There were double doors at the end of the hallway marking the entrance to a main room of some kind. The wooden doors were painted red with golden flowers and foliage designed to wrap around the top and edges. *This must be it,* he thought. Kenji brought his hand up to push the door open slowly.

"Good evening." A voice behind Kenji made him startle. "May I ask what you're doing up here? It's awfully late." The voice came from a young woman.

Kenji turned to face the person who had snuck up on him. It was indeed a young woman who looked about his age. She was standing about five feet away from him with her hands planted on her hips, looking directly into his eyes.

"Excuse me, did you hear my question? I asked what you're doing up here?" The girl asked. Kenji let go of the door and rolled his eyes.

"I came from downstairs. I was asked to make sure this door was no longer creaking. I came to fix the hinges."

Fix the hinges, what are you talking about Kenji? he thought.

"I don't recognize you. If you're from downstairs why aren't you in uniform instead of that silly costume?" the girl prodded.

"This is more comfortable to work in," he replied.

You're scrambling Kenji.

"The last time I used the door it seemed to work fine," the girl replied. "Come with me." She commanded more than asked, clearly expecting Kenji to follow.

Seeing no other option, Kenji obeyed, following the girl into a side room. The room was well lit with hanging lanterns similar to the ones in the room he saw earlier. Kenji could see the girl clearly now. She looked a little younger than him. She wore a blue silk dress with an imprint of a swan on the bottom. Her black hair was cut short but remained wavy, her bangs curling around her forehead and ears. She stood at the centre of the room now facing Kenji, her hand outstretched.

"I'm Hanako," she said with a smile.

"Kenji." He shook Hanako's hand.

"Have you come to kill Mitsunari?"

"What?" Kenji took a step back, baffled by the abruptness of the question.

"I don't know much about the politics of this war, but I know Mitsunari is vital to Sekigahara's defence. So, it would only make sense for Tokugawa to try and have him killed. So, did you come here to kill Mitsunari?"

"If you think I did, then why haven't you called the guards?" Kenji asked.

"Who says I haven't?" Hanako replied turning to look out the window.

"Who are you? A servant or a maid?" Kenji questioned.

"What concern is it to you?"

"How long do I have before soldiers come through that door?" Kenji glanced at the door.

"I don't know. A couple of minutes maybe." Hanako sat down on a chair near the corner of the room.

"So. I should probably get going then?"

"You could, or you could stay and we could talk more." Hanako was leaning forward in her chair now. "Where are you from?"

Kenji moved to the window inspecting how high he was from the nearest rooftop.

"Just a small village, nowhere important."

"So why are you involved in this war?"

"I'm not." Kenji took out his two smoke bombs and hooked them on his belt.

"It would seem otherwise."

"This is not my fight. I'm only here to fulfill a contract."

“Now I’m really interested.” Hanako stood up again and walked over to Kenji.

“You really shouldn’t be.” Kenji pulled open the door to the balcony.

“So was the contract to kill Mitsunari?”

“That looks like it’s off the table now.”

“I suppose you’re right. How were you going to do it?”

“You ask a lot of questions.” Kenji tightened his satchel over his shoulder.

“I’m curious. It’s so boring in this city. I never have anything to do.”

“I’m sure you’ll make do.” Kenji could hear the footsteps in the hallway. He started to walk on to the balcony.

“Are you going back to the camp behind the hill now?”

Kenji stopped, turning to look at Hanako.

“I never said anything about a camp.”

“I heard some of the guards talking about it. I would hurry back if I were you.”

Loud knocking could be heard coming from the hallway, followed up by a man’s voice.

“Open up! You’re outnumbered! Surrender now!”

“Looks like it’s time for you to go. It was nice to meet you, Kenji.” Hanako sat back down and watched Kenji climb on top of the railing.

“Likewise.” Kenji said as he jumped from the balcony.

It was too high for Kenji to land on his feet, so as he got close to the shingles of the nearby roof he tucked his right shoulder into his left knee, rolling over and back up onto his feet. He continued at a sprint across the rooftops being careful not to lose his balance. The buildings around him were lit up now. It seemed as if every guard in the city was aware of his presence. He knew he needed to make it to the wall on the other end of the city in the spot where he had left his rope suspended. He jumped another gap and looked down toward the street. The guards were on to him. Dozens of men were flooding the streets, running below him trying to keep up. Suddenly Kenji heard a snap that sounded like wood breaking. He skidded to a halt and crouched down. Reaching down he picked up the object that made the sound.

Arrows. He said to himself.

No time to stop. Kenji kept running toward the wall. He could hear the arrows now whizzing past his head, missing by mere inches. But he could see the wall now. Kenji made sure to control his breathing as he came to the last jump before the wall. He glanced to the sides; soldiers were converging on the wall on either side of him. It was going to be tight. Reaching the end of the roof, Kenji jumped, reaching for the concrete wall. His hands latched onto the surface of the wall and he pulled himself up.

"Freeze!"

The soldiers he saw had beaten him there. Men on either side of him wielding swords and bows, their eyes fixed on him.

"It's over, you've lost. Surrender now." A soldier shouted.

Kenji could not take them all on, there were too many. Instead he dropped his hand to his belt.

"Walk to me slowly, no sudden movements."

Kenji began to walk toward the man except he did make a sudden movement. His hand clutched the metal sphere and he threw it into the ground. The capsule split in half releasing a thick cloud of black smoke. Some of the men began to cough and others began scattering around, reaching out trying to find their bearings. Kenji had to move fast. He knelt down and felt around for the rope on the edge of the wall. He scrambled around until his hand felt rope. Grabbing tight he climbed over the wall and slid down the rope using his feet to brace against the wall. As he touched down Kenji could hear the confusion of the guards. They were all yelling trying to call out positions. Ignoring the rope burn on his hands from the fast descent, Kenji ran back to the edge of the forest. The man who brought him there had remained by the tree and grinned as Kenji approached.

"I take it they noticed you were there?"

"I may have been spotted, but we have a bigger problem. They know where the camp is. They could mass up at any moment."

"We best get moving then."

The man led the way as they both took off in the direction of Tokugawa's camp.

CHAPTER 6

Kenji and the soldier arrived back to see the camp in flames. The smoke rose above the hill as Kenji and the soldier ran to the crest. Soldiers from Sekigahara were advancing on the camp but had yet to burn all of it. The soldier unsheathed his sword and began running into the camp.

"Come on!" he yelled. Kenji looked down at the knife hung from his belt.

"Great." He took off after the soldier. Kenji ran down into the camp. The soldiers had not gotten to the centre yet, so there was still hope. Kenji ran up behind a soldier, and gripping his shoulder, slit his throat with his knife. As the man's body fell to the grass Kenji picked up his sword and continued into the camp. Kenji was met by four more soldiers, two of whom were fighting another man.

"Maku!" Kenji called out.

Maku was struggling to hold off the two men. Kenji met the strike of one soldier with his sword and kicked him to the ground. The other man rushed at him, and Kenji parried his strike and drove his sword through the man's stomach. The first man began to get up, but Kenji gave him a hard kick to the jaw, snapping the man's neck. Maku managed to kill one soldier with a slash across the chest but got a cut across his left arm because of it. Holding his arm, Maku held up his sword, preparing for the man's next strike. But Kenji came up behind him first, cutting him across the back of his knees causing him to collapse to the ground, and with one swing he cleaved the soldiers head clean off and saw it roll off to the side as his lifeless body slumped down.

"Kenji, good timing!"

"Maku, your arm. You need to get it wrapped up."

"I will, but first we need to quell this attack. Kenji, they came out of nowhere, shot arrows with fire first. They lit up the sky."

"We should get to the command tent. Make sure your lord is still breathing."

"Right, good idea." Maku's eyes were darting from side to side.

"I need you with me on this one, can I count on you?" Kenji put his hand on Maku's uninjured arm.

"Uh yes, yes. You can count on me."

"Alright good. Let's get going." Kenji led Maku back to his tent where more men were fighting outside.

"We can take these ones. Follow me." Kenji rushed toward the men.

Maku followed him and swung for one man's head. Kenji impaled a soldier but struggled to remove the sword from his stomach. Seeing another attack behind him, Kenji turned to face it and ducked underneath the swing of the soldier's sword. He gave the man a strong kick to his knee and followed it with a swift roundhouse kick to the man's jaw knocking him unconscious. Maku cut his opponent's throat, and turned to call out to Kenji.

"Kenji, look out!" The last man was running at Kenji with his sword up in the air.

"Kenji here!" Kenji's short sword came flying toward him and he snagged it out of the air. As soon as he felt the hilt, Kenji extended his arm and the man came running face first through the steel blade. Kenji lifted up his foot and pushed the now dead soldier off of his sword.

"Thanks, Maku."

"It wasn't me Kenji," Maku looked to the side. Kenji turned and saw Ichiro standing beside him.

"Ichiro!" Kenji ran up and hugged his uncle.

"Alright now." Ichiro said patting Kenji on the back.

"Where have you been?" Kenji asked frantically.

"We will discuss that later - right now we need to finish this fight. The soldiers surprised us but we now have the upper hand. If we push them back from the command tent then we should be able to end this."

"Lead the way Uncle." Ichiro turned and ran through some rubble in the direction of Tokugawa's tent. Kenji went after him, followed closely by Maku.

As they reached the command tent there were dozens of men fighting outside of it. Tensu was holding off three men with Tokugawa's samurai fighting two of their own.

"Let's go!" Ichiro commanded.

Ichiro began fighting one soldier and got locked into a grapple. Maku rushed in after and tackled another soldier to the ground. Kenji went to help Tensu who was getting overwhelmed by his three opponents. Kenji grabbed the shoulders of one man and pulled him to the ground, turning to impale him with his sword. Tensu's sword connected with another soldier and he dug his heel in to keep his ground. The third soldier was now aware of Kenji and turned to strike at his shoulder. Kenji blocked that strike and punched for the man's jaw. The soldier managed to get his forearm up to block it but Kenji followed up with a left hook to the other side of the man's face. With a splintering crack in his neck the man dropped to the grass. Kenji turned to Tensu, who had pushed his opponent back and now was on the offensive. He struck at him wildly always switching sides. That broke down the soldier's defence and with one more blow he'd cut into the top of the man's head.

"Go check on him." Tensu said motioning toward the tent.

"Can you handle it out here?"

"We will be fine." Tensu pointed to the samurai who were fighting off a group of men.

One samurai was blocking an attack while he kicked another soldier toward his partner. That soldier went flying into the extended blade of the second samurai and that samurai turned to face his partner's opponent. Without a verbal cue the first samurai ducked as his partners sword came flying and impaled his opponent's skull.

"Right yes. I'll go check on him." Kenji said.

Kenji ran inside the command tent and saw Tokugawa behind his desk, sword raised. A large man clad in heavy armour was on the other side of his desk. *Must be their leader,* he thought. Kenji ran into the room, sword at the ready. The leader turned and backhanded Kenji to the ground before he could begin a strike. Turning to Tokugawa the man struck for his head over the desk. Tokugawa blocked the strike and countered with another to the opposite side, pushing the man back. Angered, the man grabbed the desk and flung it into Tokugawa, causing him to stumble back. The man charged at Tokugawa and drove his shoulder into his chin. Tokugawa was not fazed. He kneed his opponent in the groin, causing him to recoil. Tokugawa jumped forward and connected with a flying punch to the man's jaw. As he got his footing, Tokugawa looked right at Kenji and drove his sword back behind him into the stomach of his outmatched opponent. Kenji tried not to react to the fight he had just seen. Instead he stood and faced Tokugawa.

"It seems as though the enemy is on the back foot outside. We should have this fight won as the sun rises."

"Good. Once we finish them, reconvene with Tensu and I, here in the tent. Bring your uncle."

"As you wish." Kenji left without a glance back. Outside the fighting had decreased. Maku came running to Kenji.

"Kenji! They're retreating over the hill. I think we've won."

"Great. You fought well today Maku."

"Thank you." Maku beamed.

"Go check the dead. I have to speak with Tensu and my uncle."

"Yes sir." Maku left in a hurry.

"Uncle! Tensu! Tokugawa wants to see us in his tent," Kenji called. Tensu rushed inside the tent. Ichiro rolled his eyes as he followed him inside. Kenji could not help but smile as he followed behind his uncle.

Tokugawa was sitting behind the now overturned remains of his desk with the body of his fallen opponent still blanketing the entrance. Tensu stood at attention facing Tokugawa, and Ichiro stood to his right, arms resting by his sides. Kenji came in and joined the room by standing off to the left corner.

"The enemy attack has been fought off, sir. The enemy is in full retreat," Tensu proudly announced.

"How did they surprise us?" Tokugawa questioned.

"It must have been a breakdown in the sentries my lord. I will have my men check for any casualties on the border."

"Very well. I will hold a meeting tomorrow morning, addressing our soldiers. For now, we must plan our next course of action."

Ichiro stepped forward.

"Tokugawa, if I may, the men will need their rest tonight if we are going to plan an attack sometime soon."

"You said 'we'. Does that mean you will be joining us, Ichiro?"

"I believe I am too far involved in this to not be."

"Good answer. I agree the men need rest. They can have their victory tonight and train tomorrow. The day after tomorrow, we march on Sekigahara."

"Agreed. We cannot let them muster their forces," Tensu said.

Kenji stepped forward.

"How do you plan on breaching the walls? It was quite the task climbing over them and they are thick and solid."

"Not to mention the archers that will have easy sightlines of our men," Ichiro added.

"We need not go through the wall if we can get through the gate," Tensu said.

"That would create too much of a chokepoint. Our soldiers will be cut down going through the gate all at once," Ichiro argued.

"Our cavalry will lead the charge. They will be too fast to hit effectively and they will scatter the first line of defence inside the wall," Tokugawa said now standing up from his seat. "We will lead with our foot soldiers and pike men, followed by our archers. Once our pike men have cleared an opening in their lines, our cavalry will begin their charge to break their ranks."

"A solid plan sir - shall I prepare the men?" Tensu asked.

"No, as I said, let them have their victory tonight. Tomorrow they will prepare and train."

"As you wish, sir."

"Now, let me have a minute alone with Kenji."

"Yes sir." Tensu bowed and left the room.

Ichiro glanced at Kenji and turned to leave.

"I take it your mission was unsuccessful?" Tokugawa asked.

"There were complications."

"Being?"

Kenji knew he could not tell Tokugawa he was stopped by a girl in the hallway. But he felt as if Tokugawa could look right into his mind.

"I was caught on the top floor of his house. I was lucky to make it out alive."

"Hmph, very well." Tokugawa sat back in his chair.

Kenji was surprised; he did not seem to be angry.

"Did the smoke bombs work?"

"They did, I needed to use one to escape off the top of the wall."

"Good, good. I will have to thank the quartermaster for that."

Kenji could not imagine him thanking anyone for anything.

"So, you'll be joining us in the attack?"

"It seems that way, yes."

"Very well. I saw you fight one of my men. You should be able to hold your own."

"I intend to."

To Kenji's surprise it looked like Tokugawa smiled briefly at his comment.

"I am sure you will be happy to know all of your equipment has been returned and placed in your tent."

"Thank you."

"Now Kenji, one more thing."

"Yes?"

"I'm sure Ichiro has told you that he and I know each other from our military backgrounds."

"Yes, he did tell me about that."

"How long have you known Ichiro?"

"I've known him my whole life. He helped to raise me."

"I see. Who is he to you?"

"He's my uncle, brother to my mother."

"Very well." Tokugawa did not seem satisfied with the answer. "And where is your mother?"

Kenji's fist tightened and he held back the emotion starting to build.

"She is dead, killed along with the rest of my village, nine years ago."

"In Ikebe."

"Yes."

"Kenji you must know it was nothing personal against you or your family. In war there are casualties."

"It was a long time ago." Kenji fought back the urge to climb over his desk.

"Do you miss your mother?"

"Like I said, it was a long time ago."

"Very well."

"If you'll excuse me, I haven't eaten in a while. I think I'll go join my uncle."

"As you wish." Tokugawa waved Kenji out and folded his hands in front of his chin.

CHAPTER 7

Kenji came out of the tent to a wartorn camp. Some of the fires were still blazing and bodies from both sides were being carried off to either be buried or tossed outside of camp. Kenji looked to the ground and replays of the fighting began to take place in his mind. His visual memories were interrupted by someone calling his name. It was Maku, now with a bandaged arm, running to greet him.

"Kenji! You're back. Ichiro was asking for you, said you should meet him by the mess tent."

"Thank you Maku. How's your arm?"

"It will be okay. Pretty impressive story though, right?" Maku smiled.

"Definitely. I should go find my uncle."

"Alright, I'll see you later Kenji."

Kenji waved goodbye to Maku and began walking toward the mess tent. Despite the recent attack, the camp seemed to be functioning. Soldiers moved about, training with each other or on wooden dummies, bringing food and clothing back and forth, and soldiers being treated for injuries in several open tents. In each tent he passed, Kenji saw either soldiers being treated for injuries, or those sharing a solemn drink around the fire for their fallen brothers.

When Kenji made it to the mess tent it was a different scene, filled with soldiers who could enjoy the victory and were happy to do so with others. Drinks were being passed around and jokes were being told. Laughter filled the area, even on the brink of tomorrow's battle. Kenji could not help but smile to himself. He surveyed the scene looking for his uncle. Out of the main crowd in the centre, a hand popped up and Kenji saw it belonged to Ichiro. Kenji moved through the soldiers making his way toward Ichiro.

"You made it. Maku is a good kid." Ichiro passed Kenji a drink as he sat down.

"I'm good uncle, thanks." Kenji passed the drink back over to Ichiro. "And yes, Maku seems alright."

Ichiro took a sip of Kenji's drink. "It is a shame young people have to be involved in this kind of work."

"He cannot be any younger than me Uncle; and look at me. I turned out just fine."

Ichiro laughed and almost choked on his drink.

"I'm sorry Uncle, did I say something funny?" Kenji was equal parts concerned and amused.

"No no, nothing at all. You turned out very well." Ichiro's smile grew.

"So, Uncle, are you going to tell me where you ran off to before?"

"I can assure you I did not run off anywhere."

"Uncle, I hadn't seen you for almost two days."

"You are right, I know. I should not have left like that."

"So where did you go? They would not have let you out of the camp."

"I was with Tokugawa."

"Okay. That's it?"

"We were planning."

"Planning? What could you be planning with him? You said this was not our fight."

"It is not. But there comes a time when you must pick a side. We have been on the fence for too long."

"What makes you sure this is the right side?"

"I am not sure it is. But it is the winning side."

Kenji looked around at the tables of men sharing stories and drinks. He wondered how many would be left after this war was over.

"Uncle, in the city, I was caught."

"Well it was not an easy job. How did it happen?"

Kenji paused.

"There was this girl."

"A girl? Oh Kenji."

"No, Uncle." Kenji laughed. "She questioned me as I was going to open the door."

"And this somehow stopped you from completing the task?"

Ichiro had put down his drink and had his arms crossed over the table.

"What was I supposed to do? I could not kill her."

"Was she a maid?"

"I think so. Must've been why she was in the hallways so late."

"It is good you made it out alive."

Kenji chuckled.

"What did Tokugawa think?" his uncle asked.

"He took it well. Almost like the result didn't really matter in the end."

"He is a hard man to read. He seems to have taken an interest in you. Be careful around him."

"Why do you think that is, Uncle?"

"I am not entirely sure." Ichiro seemed deep in thought for a moment before changing subjects. "It is getting late. We should rest."

"I think you're right. It's been a long day."

"That it has."

Ichiro took a last sip of his drink and the two stood up. Stretching his back, Kenji led the way out of the mess tent and back toward their tent. The sky was darkening, but the camp was illuminated by the glow of the full moon. It almost made the lit lamps seem like they were not needed. The pair walked back to the tent in silence. Upon arriving at their tent, Ichiro got undressed and began to wash his face. Kenji removed his shirt but winced when trying to lift it over his head. There was dark bruising on his abdomen, most likely a result of his rolling across rooftops earlier on.

"Did a tree fall on you?" Ichiro asked, looking over to Kenji.

"Sort of feels like it. This was from some jumping on the rooftops in Sekigahara."

"You do know you are supposed to land on your feet when you jump?"

"That was the plan."

"Poorly executed plan."

"Alright. Get your rest old man."

Ichiro climbed into bed.

"You sure you do not need me to kiss it better?"

Kenji took the empty wooden rice bowl from the night before and threw it toward Ichiro.

"Alright, message received." Ichiro turned over in his bed.

Kenji lay down in his bed but his eyes remained open. There was a thought he could not shake and it had been lingering in his mind since the city. Who was the girl and why was he even thinking about her? *Why was she in that part of the house?* He thought. His mind wandered to her blue dress. *She was dressed too nicely to be a maid. But then who was she?* Kenji could not come up with answer, but that was not what was keeping him up. It was how he could not stop thinking about her. He pictured her shining black hair falling softly around her face. Her kind but piercing eyes, with a look that both calmed and unnerved him. *That's a dangerous combination,* he thought. He told himself none of this mattered because he would not see her again. He knew the citizens of the city would flee if they won the battle and if they lost then he would not get inside the city again. Kenji raised his arms above his head creating a new pillow for himself. He needed to keep a clear head if he was going to properly prepare for this battle he and Ichiro had found themselves in. Kenji closed his eyes and fell asleep quickly with a half smile on his face.

CHAPTER 8

The morning began with the rise of the sun and the shouting of commands. Kenji sat up and listened to the invigorated camp around him. The sounds of sergeants shouting filled the camp. Kenji got dressed and went outside to witness the training underway. It was hectic, with men running back and forth carrying supplies from tent to tent and leaders drilling their soldiers. Kenji walked up to Ichiro who was observing a group of soldiers being drilled by a sergeant. They were being instructed to raise their swords over their heads and swing them down in front of them while stepping forward to add power to their strikes.

"They have been at this for hours." Ichiro said as he noticed Kenji move to his side. "And they have looked like this for hours."

"You don't think they're ready Uncle?"

"No. I think they are over confident. They think their numbers will win them this fight."

"And you think that's getting to their heads?"

"I do. It is going to get many of them killed."

"All we have to do is live through tomorrow."

Ichiro looked to Kenji with something unreadable in his eyes. "I wanted to avoid getting you into all of this Kenji."

"Is this not what you've been training me for?"

"I have been training you because you need to be able to defend yourself. I never wanted you to become a part of this war."

"This will decide the fate of Japan. Perhaps it was inevitable."

"Perhaps."

The drilling soldiers had switched positions and were now practicing jabbing toward the stomach area with their blades.

"Are your swords still in the tent?" Ichiro asked.

"Yes, resting by the bed. I was going to sharpen them later on."

"I can sharpen them for you. I was going to work on mine as well."

"Thank you, Uncle."

"Not to worry." Ichiro walked off toward their tent as Kenji continued to watch the soldiers train.

His mind shifted to thinking about the girl in Sekigahara but he dismissed the thought quickly. He made his way to the mess tent to look for something to eat. On his way there Kenji passed more groups of soldiers going over more of the same drills and sergeants yelling out the same orders. This atmosphere was all new to him. He could remember some of the soldiers in Ikebe training in the mornings, but this was on a much larger scale. Ikebe was always peaceful and the soldiers were always kind toward Kenji, some even stopping to greet him as he passed by. Here all the soldiers had determined and focused looks in their eyes, and none of them paid any attention to him as he passed by. They were focused on only one thing. War. Kenji arrived to a mostly empty mess tent. He greeted the man behind the counter and received some steamed rice with vegetables. He sat at the counter and began to eat his rice, letting his vegetables cool down a little first.

"Are you excited about the fight tomorrow?" The man behind the counter was addressing Kenji.

"Excuse me?" Kenji looked to the man, confused. How could he be excited about it?

"Most of the men say they are excited to bring the fight to the enemy tomorrow."

"Ah, I see. Well, they don't know the truth about war." Kenji replied, eating the cooled vegetables.

"I could not agree more. I would be out there as well, but I have been put back here on account of my arm."

Kenji looked up at the man and realised what he meant. The man had served him with his right arm, the only arm he had. He hadn't even noticed at first.

"I'm sorry."

"This was a long time ago now. I did my time in war, you will not see me crying about not having to go back out there."

"Do you mind if I ask how it happened?"

"Not at all, it wasn't a very heroic story. I was on the battlefield outside of a village we were attacking, and a soldier squared up to me for a one on one. He injured my arm badly, but I took more from him. I was lucky to have my fellow soldiers near me. They carried me away from the battle, and in the morning I found out they had to amputate. Not the most comforting thing to wake up to."

"That's terrible."

"Ah, well. As I said, it was a long time ago. Now I just get to listen to all the cocky soldiers talk about their excitement regarding this war. They're in for a shock I tell you."

"Yes, they are." Kenji ate the last of his food and handed the bowl back to the man. The man knelt down and put the bowl behind the counter.

"I wish you luck tomorrow." The man said holding his hand out to Kenji. "I'm Taku by the way."

Kenji held out his hand to meet the man's handshake. "Kenji. And thanks for the luck and the meal."

"My pleasure, Kenji."

Kenji stood and left, thinking on the man's story. He hoped luck would help him tomorrow. He looked down and realised he was rubbing his left arm. He went out looking for Ichiro, when he heard shouts coming from behind him. Going to investigate, Kenji saw the noise was coming from a horse, unhappy about being saddled. Two soldiers were holding up the saddle trying to position it on the horse's back while a third man was holding the reins in an attempt to hold the horse steady. The horse was not pleased however and was bucking wildly trying to thwart the men's attempts.

"What's going on here?" Kenji questioned the man holding the reins.

"It's his mind, the horse has seen too much war. He does not want anymore."

"What's his name?"

"His name is Sutoraidā, Strider."

"Let me help."

Kenji stepped up to the horse and put out his hand. The horse continued to buck, nervous about the new face. Kenji inched forward slowly careful not to frighten the horse more than he already was.

"It's alright boy, it's okay."

The horse kept to the ground now but continued to back away from Kenji's outstretched arm. He persisted moving ever closer to Strider.

"Give me the reins." Kenji insisted moving his other arm out to reach for them. The soldier moved toward Kenji and passed him the reins before backing away. Kenji held out the reins for Strider to see.

"Look it's alright, I'm not pulling. You have to work with me Sutoraidā."

Strider started to calm but neighed loudly and continued to move away from him.

"It's okay, boy." Kenji moved closer now, his hand only inches away from his neck.

Strider lowered his head but stopped retreating. He was breathing heavily but no longer bucking.

"That's it. You're okay." Kenji reached out and touched Strider's neck, his hand tiny in comparison to the horse's large body. Strider neighed again but did not back away. Instead he turned his head away from Kenji. "You see. I'm not that bad."

Kenji caressed his neck, rubbing slowly and stepping closer to him. He was a beautiful animal. His cream mane ran the length of his brown neck. He was tall and strong and very proud because of it. He allowed Kenji to touch him but refused to look at him.

"Put it on." Kenji gestured to the men still holding the saddle above their heads.

The men crept forward, slowly placing the saddle atop Strider. Strider neighed again but did not move. It was as if Kenji's touch kept him glued to his place. Strider relaxed again as the men strapped on the saddle. Kenji handed the reins back to the man and patted Strider on the shoulder.

"Be gentle." Kenji advised as he walked away.

CHAPTER 9

Kenji rubbed his hands as he looked around for the weaponsmith, hoping to see Ichiro. It was midday now, and the sun was beating down on the camp. Kenji was only in light clothing from head to toe but he still felt the heat. The soldiers had a worse time of it. Most of them were required to wear their armour and carry around their weapons in case of an attack or being called suddenly into battle. Some men were clearly struggling with the heat, breathing heavily and sweating. Others did their best to hide their discomfort. Kenji turned as he heard the clang of metal, telling him he must be getting close to the weaponsmith.

"Something I can help you with?"

The man behind the anvil addressed Kenji. He was a strong man, built like a water buffalo, suited to the physicality of his job.

"An older man came by here earlier to sharpen some swords. I was wondering if you knew where he went."

"Sorry, I'm not sure. It was over an hour since he was here. The swords he brought me were of high quality. Didn't take me long to sharpen them up. Were they yours?"

"Two of them."

"Be sure you take good care of them. Very fine weapons they were."

"I will." Kenji turned to leave.

"It looked like he was heading toward the commander's tent," the man called out.

Kenji looked back over his shoulder and gave a nod.

"Thank you."

As Kenji left, he noticed stacks of wooden boards and logs piled to the side of the blacksmiths tent. *Probably for stoking the fires,* he thought. Kenji made his way to Tokugawa's tent but as he walked his mind drifted again. He thought about tomorrow and the coming battle. Kenji had fought before, more times than he liked, but this was different. There were going to be more people around him tomorrow than he had ever seen in one place. Some of them were going to try and kill him, but even more of them were going to be fighting with him. He hoped it would be enough. As he walked to the entrance of the tent, Kenji looked at the two samurai who he watched fight the night before. Their armour and weapons were cleaned, and they looked as if nothing had happened. They stood at attention as Kenji entered. He looked in toward Tokugawa's office, and there was Ichiro joined by Tensu.

"Enter, Kenji." Tokugawa waved his arm, gesturing him forward.

Kenji stood off to the side behind Ichiro. Ichiro had their swords still hung over his shoulder.

"We are just discussing the final preparations for the attack tomorrow."

Ichiro spoke up.

"I agree with your plan to take the entrance gate, but there is still the problem of our approach. Their soldiers will surely meet us out in the field as a show of power and it will be effective if they are backed by their archers on the wall."

Tensu stepped forward slightly.

"Our forces outnumber theirs. We will take the city by force and skill. Our horses will be hard to hit, as you said last night, sir."

"But our soldiers are easy targets, especially in an open field. They need cover." Ichiro retorted.

"Yes, but where will we find cover in an open field?" Tokugawa looked at Ichiro.

Kenji thought back to the wooden boards piled by the blacksmith.

"Sir, if I may." Kenji stepped forward now. "As I left the blacksmith on the way here, I noticed a large pile of boards stacked outside."

"And how will that help us?" Tensu questioned.

Kenji gave him a sharp look and continued.

"Surely we must have more wood throughout the camps. Perhaps we can make our own cover."

Tokugawa leaned forward now on his knees. His desk was now gone, damaged from the fight last night.

"You are suggesting portable cover?"

"Yes. It may not be sturdy but at least it will be something between our men and their archers. We will just have to carry them far enough to engage their defending force."

"He may be right. If we can get close enough, their archers will not risk firing as much if it is into their own forces." Ichiro said.

"Tensu, can the men have enough of these barriers built by tomorrow to cover our lines?"

"It shall be done sir. I will have my men get started right away."

"Good. We all know the plan for tomorrow then?" Tokugawa addressed the room now.

"I believe we do." Ichiro said.

Kenji and Tensu nodded in agreement.

"Then Tensu, start your men on building as many barriers as they can. Ichiro and Kenji, get the rest you need, I expect you on the frontline tomorrow."

Tensu and Kenji bowed and the trio left the tent to go their separate ways.

"Uncle, are you ready for tomorrow?" Kenji asked as they walked back to their tent under the setting sun.

"Am I ready? I should be asking you."

"You are getting older. I just want to make sure you can keep up." Kenji smiled as he held open the tent flap for his uncle to walk in.

"Boy, I have been doing this for a long time. I am going to be right there beside you tomorrow." Ichiro sat on the edge of his bedroll. "So I can hold your hand."

This time Kenji laughed as he sat across from his uncle on the other bed.

"Do you think we have a chance to win tomorrow?" Kenji's grin faded slightly at his own question.

"I think we will come out of it alive. I am not sure anyone will be a victor at the end of this war."

"So why fight then, Uncle? If no one wins, why do people always fight?"

"Kenji, that is a question I wish I had the answer to. Wars have been fought over many things. Power, wealth, control. History will always record a victor, but the part it does not record is the right and wrong."

"But then how does history ever write a side as the right side?

"It is all a matter of perspective. The people of Sekigahara believe they are good, fighting the good fight. Tokugawa's soldiers think the same of themselves."

"So, we're not on the right side or the wrong side?"

"Kenji, there is still much you must learn about war. There is always more grey area. It is never black and white. The best you can ever do is stick to your own morals."

"But how do we know if our morals are the right ones?"

Ichiro sighed and leaned back.

"I wish I had the answer. The best you can do is fight with honour and do what you feel in your heart is the right thing. But enough about that, I am going to find us something to eat." Ichiro stood and left the tent, leaving Kenji to ponder their conversation in silence. Kenji took his swords and hung them on a chair next to his bed. He winced slightly as he bent back down, and rubbed his side where the bruise had formed. Next time he would land on his feet. Stretching his back now, Kenji went to the bowl of water and cupped his hands, scooping some up to splash his face. The water was colder than he expected and he grabbed a cloth to dry with. Shadows were beginning to grow inside the tent as the sun crept behind the horizon. He sat down on the chair his swords were now hung on and he heard the sound of soldiers working outside. The banging of wood and the clang of metal told Kenji that work had begun on the barriers he had suggested. Suddenly, he could smell an aroma coming toward the tent. It was followed closely by Ichiro who had returned with two bowls of soup.

"Here you are." Ichiro handed Kenji one of the bowls and returned to his spot on the bed opposite him.

"Thanks." Kenji hastily began eating the soup, not realizing how hungry he was.

"Kenji, whatever happens tomorrow you stay close to me alright?"

"Yes, of course. I need to keep an eye on you."

Ichiro smirked. "Yes, sure you do."

The pair finished their soup in silence.

CHAPTER 10

Kenji awoke to rustling inside his tent. He sat up quickly and reached for his sword startling the woman who was the cause of the noise.

"Are you not happy to see me? Follow me."

Kenji was still groggy. His eyes were having trouble adjusting to the darkness. He stumbled out of bed, past a sleeping Ichiro, and followed the woman out of the tent. The moonlit sky gave Kenji enough light to follow the outline of the tent and make his way behind it. As he turned the corner he came face to face with the intruder, their noses almost touching. Startled, Kenji took a small step back.

"Hanako?" Kenji almost shouted the name. "What are you doing here? If one of the soldiers sees you, you will be killed!"

"Are you worried about me?" Hanako was surprisingly calm.

"Well, a little, yes. What do you want?"

"You're attacking tomorrow? The camp seems to be preparing for an attack."

"Why?"

"I don't know why you're attacking. There are a lot of innocent people in the city."

"You know that's not what I meant. Why are you asking? Why are you here?"

"I wanted to make sure you know not everyone in the city has to die."

"You cannot stop this attack. It's too late now."

"I know, but I want to save as many people as I can."

"You're not a maid, are you?"

"Ha." Hanako chuckled quietly. "Is that what you thought I was?"

"To be honest, I was a bit distracted." Kenji argued.

"By me, or by your very secret mission?" Hanako smiled. Kenji rolled his eyes.

"You should leave."

"You're not very courteous, are you?"

"Sorry I didn't welcome you with open arms."

"I'll leave. Just remember there are innocents in war."

Hanako left without another word leaving Kenji pondering the reality of the situation. He walked back inside the tent and laid down. He needed all the rest he could get before tomorrow. He did not sleep another minute.

The next morning was once again filled with the sounds of men rushing about, except this time there was something different in the air. It was equal parts eagerness and tension. Kenji thought the tension outweighed the eagerness.

"You look tired." Ichiro handed Kenji some clothes.

"Oh, thanks." Kenji took the clothes from his uncle as he tried to wipe the sleep from his eyes.

"A soldier came in and told me we move out as the sun passes over the hill."

"Cannot wait."

"Are you ready for this?" Ichiro put a hand on Kenji's shoulder.

"Yes, I'm fine. Just a bad sleep, but I'm alright."

"Okay then." Ichiro turned to leave. "A soldier left some armour for you on the chair." Ichiro gestured to the chair that held a wooden breast plate with wrist and shoulder guards to match.

"Where's yours then?"

"I get the glory of wearing a captain's uniform, by request of the great Tokugawa." Ichiro waved his hands in the air as he left the tent.

Kenji smiled to himself as he began to put on his clothes. As he sat to tie on the armour he thought about the night before. He would need to suppress those thoughts today. He could not afford to be distracted. The armour was rigid and restricting. It might save his life but Kenji felt like he could not move in it. As he stood up, he tried to adjust it but without success. He left the tent with his swords strapped on his back and the remaining smoke bombs on his belt. The sun had begun to creep over the horizon painting the sky in a wash of pink and yellow. Kenji's moment of serenity was interrupted by the shouts of captains giving orders to soldiers rushing to the hill. The whole camp was alive and preparing to gather at the hill on the border. Kenji fell into line behind a group of men passing by his tent. They were in tight formation, almost crushing Kenji between them. Kenji was bumped by one soldier to his left and turned his head in response. To his surprise, he was staring into the eyes of the man he bested in the ring earlier in the week. This time, the soldier gave Kenji a nod of respect.

"You still owe me a drink." Kenji joked.

"If we live through this, I'll buy you two." The man replied, smiling.

Kenji and the soldier followed their group to the top of the hill, and Kenji tried not to gasp. Thousands of soldiers lined the top of the hill, covering so much ground the grass beneath them was no longer visible. Kenji's group moved into position near the front of what he thought was the left of the army. Moving into line, Kenji could see the wooden defenses Tensu's builders had constructed. Large wooden boards were pieced together to create small walls carried out front by teams of men. Kenji hoped they would hold together under fire. Soldiers were still falling into line across the top of the hill as a split formed in the center. The opening revealed Tokugawa on horseback, dressed in his heavy gold edged armour. He was tailed closely by Tensu and Ichiro, riding horses of their own. Tokugawa moved to the front of the army and turned to face them. As his horse neighed, Tokugawa unsheathed his sword and raised it above his head and a cheer erupted from the soldiers like thunder from a storm. Without a word, Tokugawa turned back again to face the city of Sekigahara in the distance. *Rousing speech,* Kenji thought.

Kenji looked out to the distant city and saw opposing soldiers massing outside the high walls. It was too far for Kenji to see clearly, but he was sure archers would be lining the upper walls, each with arrows notched and drawn back. Once again, Tokugawa raised his still unsheathed sword but this time pointed it directly at the city walls. His horse began to trot and sparked the army to march. Slow and steady, the army was in sync, every step feeling as if it would shake the ground and drive creatures into their subterranean burrows. Kenji tensed as the soldiers in the distance began to get closer. Now he could see the archers, and sure enough their eyes were fixed upon them with arrows drawn back and elbows cocked high. The sun continued to rise illuminating the field in front of them as if to light their path. But the light changed to a looming shadow. Kenji looked up and realized the cause of the sudden change in light. The elbows of the archers had relaxed because their arrows now filled the sky.

"Incoming!" one of the captains near Kenji shouted.

Kenji tensed again and slightly lowered his stance as the thundering sound of the soldiers' march was replaced by their screams. Men dropped to the left and right of Kenji and he could not tell if the barricades were helping. He just needed to focus on getting to the walls. The pace of the soldiers quickened now, but none dared to run in front of the barricades until they got closer. Kenji peered over the top of the men to see Tokugawa leading the march, unflinching even as a second rain of arrows came flying toward them. This time Kenji ducked as he moved forward but was nearly knocked over as a corpse of a soldier fell back into him. Kenji shrugged off the body and kept pushing forward with the army. Now the soldiers had quickened pace again and a shout erupted from multiple captains.

"Charge!"

Just as a herd of animals gets startled and charges, Tokugawa's army exploded into a sprint with swords drawn and eyes focused on their objective. As the barriers were dropped and replaced with unsheathed weapons, Kenji reached back and grasped both of his swords. Drawing them out and off his back, Kenji joined the men in their charge and lowered his swords to his sides. All thoughts in his head were discarded as Kenji rushed toward the wall of soldiers standing between him and the city. The man who had given his respect to Kenji at the start of the march had run up alongside him and had his sword raised above his head. As both armies connected in a crash of flesh and metal, the soldier who joined Kenji was stopped in his tracks, sword locked with an opponent. Having no time to look back, Kenji focused his attention on a soldier rushing toward him. Using the momentum of his sprint, Kenji drove both his swords forward through the man's breastplate, and quickly them pulled out to duck under another incoming swing. Kenji turned to face the new threat, but the man had already dropped to the ground. Within seconds, a new threat replaced the old as another soldier lunged at Kenji. Kenji parried the man's sword with his left and swept up and across the man's throat with his right. The man collapsed as his severed trachea spurted blood onto Kenji's face. Without time to wipe his face Kenji slashed both of his swords across another soldier's back. As he fell to the grass a familiar face was revealed behind him.

"Kenji!" Maku yelled to his friend.

"Maku!" Kenji greeted him with a quick punch on the shoulder as the pair squared up against more soldiers rushing their way.

As the soldiers approached, Kenji sidestepped the first and drove his right sword behind him through the man's back and lunged forward to drive his left sword through the approaching soldier's torso. But Kenji aimed high and his blade bounced off the man's shoulder guard. The soldier took this opportunity to swing for Kenji's head as Kenji tried to pull his other sword from the stomach of the man behind him. He did not need to, as the soldier let out a cry as a result of Maku's sword piercing his shoulder blade. Now able to get his sword free, Kenji slashed the man across the chest and he went down, head crashing to the dirt. Kenji gave Maku a nod, and Maku smiled in response. The pair continued toward the wall but quickly realized they had lost sight of it. With bodies surrounding them their vision was filled with dueling soldiers.

Suddenly another man came up behind Maku and struck his shoulder. Maku fell to his knees as Kenji rushed to help his friend. Kenji raised his sword but was knocked to the ground by a soldier, and Maku was lost in the crowd. The new soldier jumped on Kenji and cleaved down at his head. Kenji crossed his swords over his face as the man's sword connected in between his own. With a swift kick to the man's groin, Kenji thrust his swords into each of the man's shoulders in between the breast plate and shoulder guards. Yanking his arms to the side Kenji took the man to the ground and rushed to his feet, frantically looking for Maku. He was nowhere to be seen. Kenji saw an opening through the crowd and rushed to close the distance. He stopped as he saw Tokugawa engaged in a three-way fight on horseback.

Tokugawa thrust his sword down into the top of one man's shoulder, dispatching him quickly. He yanked on the reins of his horse triggering a high kick in the air that knocked the second man to the ground. The soldier let out a shrill scream, interrupted as the hooves of Tokugawa's mount came crashing onto him. The last man rushed Tokugawa but fell to the dirt as Ichiro's blade pierced his back.

"Keep moving forward!" Tokugawa thrust his sword toward the gates of Sekigahara.

"Forward, Kenji!" Ichiro motioned at Kenji then toward the wall.

Kenji ran toward Ichiro and caught up with him as he was locked in a fight with another soldier. Kenji saw two more men headed toward his uncle and ran to intercept. He swung his sword upward at the first man connecting with his sword and knocking him back. The second man jabbed at Kenji as he ran toward him. Kenji sidestepped the strike, but got clipped by the blade. Kenji's right bicep instantly felt hot and he knew the solider had drawn blood. Turning his injured shoulder away from the man, Kenji struck the man's leg causing him to collapse to the ground. Kenji turned to face the attacker he had previously knocked back and raised his sword to his face to block the incoming strike. Kenji kicked high to the man's jaw, causing him to stumble and followed up by thrusting his sword through his stomach. The soldier folded over Kenji's sword before falling to the field. Kenji turned once more to finish the crippled soldier but instead dodged an incoming horse. Tokugawa dashed by, his sword sweeping down to finish Kenji's fight without losing speed. Tokugawa led the charge toward the wall, as his army, with Kenji among them, followed. Tokugawa reared his horse, its legs crashing into the gates. Archers aimed their shots directly down from the wall, their arrows causing bodies to pile at the base. More cavalry joined Tokugawa, and Kenji could hear the gate begin to creak from the power of the horses. Ichiro ran up next to Kenji, bumping him slightly from behind.

"If we breach the gates they will stand down!" Ichiro yelled over the fighting. "Come on!"

Ichiro took off toward the gates with Kenji in tow. As they arrived, the gates began to give, splintering as the horses began a charge between them. Like water crashing between rocks, soldiers flooded into the city, striking down every opponent they encountered. As Kenji got inside, he was met with the screams of men and women alike, all fleeing from the scores of men now inside their city. Kenji slowed his pace to a halt, and watched as the men he was fighting alongside pursued the civilians of Sekigahara, cutting them down in the streets. Kenji turned his ear to listen to hooves trotting up behind him.

"Walk with me Kenji." Tokugawa dismounted behind him and handed off the reins to a passing soldier. "It's on to the royal house now."

Kenji followed as they caught up with Ichiro and began walking in unison toward the house Kenji had infiltrated not long ago. As they walked the street, Kenji surveyed the ongoing attack. The defenders of Sekigahara were in full retreat, running to find shelter, leaving women and children behind. Mothers clutching their children ran past, as Tokugawa's men set fire to the buildings behind them. Only a handful of soldiers stayed back to resist the attack, trying desperately to give the civilians more time to escape. But it was futile. Sekigahara was overwhelmed - a once great city sacked within an afternoon. Kenji's cheeks felt the heat of the torched buildings beside him as they neared the doors of the royal house. Men, women and children were brought from the houses that lined the courtyard outside the royal house. Soldiers lined them up on either side of the street as they approached the doors. Tokugawa and Ichiro stopped together as Kenji stumbled, too focused on the people who were being lined up around him. Focusing ahead now, Kenji took a small step back to realign with Tokugawa and Ichiro and looked forwards toward the now open doors. Tensu stepped through, followed by a small crowd. *Must be the royal family,* Kenji thought. Four handmaids were next, wearing silk dresses that brushed the ground as they walked. Their gazes were directed at their feet. They split off to the sides as Mitsunari walked through them. His head was held high and his gaze locked onto Tokugawa. His wife followed closely behind, along with a girl who Kenji assumed must be their daughter. Both their eyes were looking at the street beneath them. They stood behind Mitsunari as Tensu approached him and put a hand to his shoulder guiding Mitsunari to his knees. Mitsunari looked up at Tokugawa, unblinking, his chin still high as if to say he was not defeated yet. Kenji looked to Ichiro, who was looking toward the family in front of them. Tokugawa stepped forward.

"Mitsunari, do you choose to die by seppuku or by my blade?"

"You have no honour in this win. If you want to defeat me you will have to give me a sword."

"You are already defeated. You and your city were the last disgrace to be dealt with. You should have sided with me and together we could have reshaped Japan."

"Your vision of Japan will never be realized. Others will stand in your way."

"But do you not see, there is no one left. Japan is mine now. So I ask you again, seppuku or my blade?"

Tokugawa brought his hand down to the hilt of his sword as his other extended toward Mitsunari, offering his knife.

"Let my family go. They will not oppose you, they have done nothing wrong."

Tokugawa was silent as he took a step toward Mitsunari further extending his arm. Mitsunari looked back toward his wife and daughter, their eyes now glued to his. Kenji could hear quiet sobbing from the wife. Mitsunari took a deep breath in as he reached out to grasp the knife from Tokugawa's palm. A silence came over the occupants of the courtyard as Mitsunari took hold of the knife with both hands. Kenji exhaled quietly not realizing he had been holding his breath. Mitsunari raised his arms out in front of his body, the knife pointed down toward him.

"I wish for a better Japan."

Mitsunari let out a grunt as he plunged the knife into his stomach. Kenji's eyes grew wide as Mitsunari's body curled over the blade and collapsed to the ground. His wife let out a cry and rushed toward Mitsunari's body. She was stopped by the firm hand of Tensu. The daughter looked at her lifeless father, her eyes red and wet. Kenji's mouth opened as he came to a realization. Hanako was standing before him having just witnessed her father's death. Crying and moaning could be heard from the surrounding crowd as soldiers lined up behind them.

"Execute them. We're done here." Tokugawa ordered.

Swords were unsheathed from the outside of the crowd and Kenji stood shocked as the bodies of men, women and children fell to the ground around him. In that moment, all Kenji could hear was the sound of life being taken away as the street was being covered in corpses. Tensu unsheathed his sword and raised it above Hanako and her mother.

"No!"

Kenji unsheathed his sword and stepped underneath Tensu's strike. Pushing back hard, Kenji blocked Tensu's sword and stood in front of Hanako.

"Kenji!" Ichiro barked. "Stand down!"

"You disappoint me, Kenji." Tokugawa said stepping up to meet him.

"This is wrong. These people are innocent and you have won."

"This is war, boy."

"Mitsunari was right, you have no honour! You should have fought him!"

"Kenji, step aside!" Ichiro ordered.

"You know nothing of war and you will never learn, because this will be your last."

Tokugawa put his hand to his sword. Kenji stood his ground. In one swift pull, Tokugawa released his sword and drew it back thrusting it toward Kenji. Kenji puffed his chest and shut his eyes waiting for the sting of the blade he knew was coming. But Kenji exhaled without pain and opened his eyes. His stare was met with the eyes of his uncle looking back at him.

"Kenji... run."

Kenji looked down and saw the bloodied tip of a sword pierced through Ichiro's stomach.

"Uncle?"

Kenji grabbed Ichiro's shoulder as he dropped to the ground.

"Uncle no! No, no please. Not now!"

Tokugawa pulled his sword back and Ichiro collapsed in Kenji's arms, his lifeless eyes staring up at him.

"Bastard!"

Kenji stood up to engage Tokugawa but was pulled back hard. Hanako had grabbed his belt at the same time, removing one of his remaining smoke bombs. Kenji was engulfed in smoke as the sphere cracked against the stone.

CHAPTER 11

~1587 - Ikebe Village~

"Uncle, do you kill bad men?" Kenji sat beside Ichiro on the grass and began to play with some leaves.

"Why would I kill anyone Kenji?"

"Well, I know it's not good to kill people, but what about bad men?"

"What about them?"

"You know, should they be killed?"

"I do not think that is for us to decide, Kenji."

"Then who decides if it's okay?"

"In war Kenji, people will die. Whether it is right or wrong, it is something that will happen. I hope you never have to make that decision for yourself."

"But Uncle?"

"Yes, my boy?"

Kenji looked down at his toes.

"What if one day you die?"

"Everyone dies Kenji, it is a part of life. My time will come one day."

"But I don't want you to die. What if a bad man kills you before you kill him?"

"Kenji, I want you to promise me something."

"What is it Uncle?"

"If I go out to fight and I do not come back I do not want you to grieve. If I do not come back from a battle it just means it will be my time."

"But shouldn't I kill a bad man if he kills you?"

Ichiro placed a hand on Kenji's shoulder.

"Kenji, I want you to listen to me very carefully. Revenge is not the right way. You cannot go after someone who has killed me."

"But why not?"

"If I am killed, I only hope it is an honourable death. And an honourable death need not be avenged."

Kenji wrapped his arms around his uncle.

"I never want you to leave."

"Kenji, I am not going anywhere anytime soon. Now I am starving. Shall we go see what is for lunch?"

"Okay, race you!"

Kenji leapt up and raced down the hill toward his house, leaving his uncle to catch up.

~1599 - Orochi Forest~

Leaves slapped against his face and branches snapped across his cheeks, drawing small cuts. But Kenji just kept running. Breathing hard, Kenji pushed farther and farther into the forest. He ducked under a low hanging branch and vaulted over a crashed log across his path. Kenji slowed to rest against the trunk of a tree, placing his hand against it for stability. His chest was heaving as his looked back over his shoulder for the first time since he started running. Civilians were metres behind him trying to keep up through the thick undergrowth of the forest. But they were not going to make it. Soldiers followed close behind, catching up to some before they could escape. Hanako's mother ran past Kenji, followed by Hanako and two other men. Kenji grabbed Hanako's bicep as she ran past.

"Keep moving, don't stop." Kenji said in between breaths. "Is there somewhere safe you can take them?"

"I can think of a place. But we'll never make it. There are too many soldiers and some of the civilians will not be able to keep up."

"I'll buy you as much time as I can. Which way is it?"

"Keep going north until you hit a creek. We'll rest there and wait for you."

"Okay, if I'm not there by sundown leave without me. Now go!"

Hanako took off after the rest of the people who had already made it past Kenji. Kenji turned to face the incoming soldiers and unsheathed the swords from his back. Holding them down by his sides he walked toward the soldiers closing in on him. He met the first soldier's sword with his own parrying first, using his other sword to slash across his throat, disposing of him quickly. Two more rushed him now, and he push kicked the first and raised his sword to his chin to block the next. Using his free hand, he plunged his sword through the soldier he had blocked, and kicked him off the blade of his sword. The man he had knocked back came at him next and Kenji drove both his swords through the man's breast plate, spinning as he pulled them out so he could quickly face the next threat.

Kenji looked to see a woman begin to lose the grasp of her child. A soldier was tugging the girl the other way. Kenji ran toward him, but the soldier saw him first. The soldier released the child to swing at Kenji with his blade, and Kenji reacted by dropping to his knees and sliding under the man's swing. As he passed him, Kenji swung his right arm back and connected with the man's calf causing him to yell out in pain and drop to his knees. As Kenji stood, he drove his sword back into the shoulder blade of the soldier. The man dropped to the grass without another sound.

"Get out of here now!" Kenji turned to look at the woman and her daughter.

"Thank you!"

The woman took her child's hand, but the girl stayed to tug on Kenji's pant leg.

"Look," she said pointing back toward the city.

A swarm of soldiers were charging toward them. Swords drawn and eyes locked to them the group closed in.

"We will not be able to outrun them. You two need to go." Kenji wiped his swords on his pants and held them up in front of him.

The woman took Kenji's wrist. "There are too many of them."

"I'll hold them back but you need to get your girl to safety." Kenji lowered his stance slightly, readying himself for the next fight.

"Look mama, over there!" The girl was pointing to a creature dashing toward them through the bushes.

"Strider!" Kenji sighed. "Quick, get on!"

Strider trotted up alongside them and waited patiently for the woman and her child to mount.

"Quickly now!" Kenji turned again to face the incoming soldiers.

The woman heaved her girl up onto Strider as Kenji blocked the first soldier to arrive. Striking him down with a blow to the chest Kenji gave the second attacker a hard side kick sending him stumbling back into his comrades.

"Here!"

Kenji turned to see the woman's outstretched hand and he sheathed his right sword to his back to grab hold. With a grunt the woman helped to hoist Kenji up with them as the soldiers continued to rush in. Kenji turned his shoulder down toward the next soldier to close in on them and thrust his sword into his chest.

"Strider, get us out of here!" Kenji gave Strider a firm pat on the neck and Strider took off into the forest.

The woman held on to Kenji's shoulders with the girl nestled between them as Strider dashed past trees and through the foliage.

"Where are the others? Were there anymore behind you?" Kenji turned his head back to address the mother.

"I don't think so. I think we were the last out. My..." The woman paused. "My husband didn't make it out."

"I'm sorry. The other survivors told me to meet them at a creek to the north. From there we were to head to a safe area together. Do you know the way?"

"Yes, I believe I do. If we keep on this path, we should catch up to them."

"Good. We will need to hurry. Tokugawa will not take long to send out his cavalry after us."

Kenji glanced behind them, half expecting the cavalry to already be on their tail. All he could see was the forest and the faint outline of the city wall getting smaller through the trees. As Strider galloped through the forest, Kenji could hear the faint sound of rushing water and the hushed chatter of people up ahead.

"Whoa Strider, up ahead."

Strider slowed his pace and began to trot up behind the remaining survivors who had huddled around the creek bed awaiting Kenji. Kenji motioned for the mother and her girl to stay on the horse and dismounted to address the group.

"Are we ready to move?"

Hanako stood up from the crowd. "Yes, we're ready. It's not far from here."

"Perfect. We don't have much time before they'll be on us again."

"You're hurt."

Hanako touched his right shoulder where he had gotten clipped by a soldier's blade during the assault on the wall. The blood had seeped through his shirt now and had begun to harden around the cut.

"No time now. We'll deal with it when we stop. You should lead, you know the way. I'll stay in the back and make sure we're a safe distance ahead."

"Alright. Everyone, this way! We need to hurry!"

The group got to their feet and proceeded to follow Hanako across the creek. Kenji waited for Strider to pass with the woman and child, and received a gracious nod from the mother with a smile to accompany it from the girl. Kenji nodded in response trying not to think about their odds of escaping Tokugawa's soldiers.

The group's pace had slowed significantly as the sun receded behind the trees to be replaced by the rising moon. The children walked the slowest, their backs hunched as they followed the adults to their unknown location. As Kenji followed, he tried to keep his mind off recent events. He knew his priority needed to be protecting this group, this band of people who had been thrown together that he was now charged with keeping safe. They did not even know him, he had just invaded their city and ruined their lives, yet they travelled with him as if they trusted him. Perhaps they did not, but were too tired to fight. He could feel it now too, the exhaustion. His muscles ached with each step he took. He winced suddenly as his right shoulder brushed into a branch of a tree. He looked at his arm, only now remembering what caused the shot of pain. There was a horizontal gash across the side of his bicep, the aftermath of the arrow that was fired at it. He had no time to worry about it now. He needed to get this group to Hanako's safe area before he could deal with it.

Kenji's mind drifted back to Ichiro. So many emotions were running through his head. He did not have long to decipher them because of a tug on his pant leg. He stopped and looked down to see a young boy reaching up to him. Kenji looked at him, puzzled, and the boy gestured with his chin to the girl and her mother atop Strider. Kenji understood the message and sighed as he knelt down in front of the boy. The child happily hopped onto his back and wrapped his legs and arms around Kenji. Kenji coughed before lowering the boy's arms to his shoulders relieving the pressure that was briefly around his neck. The boy giggled at Kenji as he regained his breath and Kenji could not help but smile back. More people within the group smiled as well and some even laughed, momentarily lifting the invisible weight off the collective shoulders of the travelling group. Kenji put his hands under the boy's legs keeping him hoisted on his back as the group carried on.

As Kenji carried his passenger past a group of trees and into a clearing, his nose caught the scent of water. The breeze caused the pond in front of them to mist their path and Kenji felt refreshed as tiny drops tickled his face.

"We're here." Hanako turned back to address the group.

A large unified breath was released from the group as they spread out to sit or lay across the grass. Kenji knelt down once again to allow the boy to clamber off and join his family near a cluster of flowers. He stood once more to survey the area Hanako had brought them to. It was a small open area about the size of the courtyard in Sekigahara. Only a few shrubs and plants were scattered around and the rest was taken up by the pond at the center, with a rock formation off to his left. The trees around them were no thicker than the rest of the forest but they would provide adequate coverage from prying eyes on the outside of the secluded area.

"Do you like it?" Hanako approached Kenji smiling, but she was clearly exhausted from the trip.

"It's nice." Kenji admitted. "You think we'll be safe here?"

"I think so. Well, I hope so. The cities patrols never went out this far anyway."

"You've been here a lot?"

"I used to come here to get away from the city sometimes. It got really noisy and they never let me wander around for too long." Hanako paused. "Oh right! There's something else, let me show you!"

She took Kenji's hand and led him toward the rock formation at the edge of the tree line.

"Here, help me move these." Hanako bent down to begin picking up branches resting against the face of the rock.

Kenji bent over to help her, and was surprised when he removed a cluster to find a hole in the rock. The rock formation was not solid, it was a cave.

"Pretty great, huh?" Hanako smiled triumphantly.

"This is great. How deep does it go?"

"Not too far but it should fit all of us. We'll just have to get more comfortable together."

Kenji put his hand up on the arch of the cave entrance to peer inside. She was right, it was not large, but would be big enough to fit their group.

"About that nasty cut," Hanako addressed his injury.

"It's from the battle. Just a small cut. Not a big deal."

"That is not a small cut. We need to clean it."

"Maybe this is not the best ti-"

"Sit." Hanako pointed to the grass. Taken off guard by the command Kenji did as she asked and sat with his back to the rock. Hanako knelt beside him and peered into the cut on his arm.

"Take this off." She gave his shirt a pull. Kenji removed his shirt and held his breath as he raised his right arm above his head. He tossed it to the side and rested again against the cave wall. Kenji took a sharp breath in, feeling the cool rock face against his skin. Hanako turned and motioned for the boy Kenji was previously carrying to join them.

"Ujimushi and sticks." Hanako told the boy and the boy hurried off to complete his task.

"Why maggots?" Kenji grimaced at the thought.

"They will clean it."

"I would rather let it get infected."

"Don't be such a baby. And what on earth is this from?" Hanako pointed to Kenji's bruised abdomen.

"I actually got that the night I met you."

"I didn't hit you, did I?" She looked up in thought.

Kenji smirked. "No, no, I got this from rolling from a fall on one of the rooftops."

"Why didn't you land on your feet?" she questioned.

"Ha, you sound just like my..." Kenji trailed off and looked down. "Look here comes your helper." Kenji pointed to the boy who had returned with full hands and a big smile across his face.

"Perfect." Hanako turned to thank the boy who had dropped the sticks he had collected at her feet and was now holding out his hands.

Inside the boy's grasp were small maggots wriggling around in his palm, as if fighting for the most comfortable spot on a bed. Kenji frowned at the sight. Hanako gave the boy a pat on the head and took the maggots from him allowing the boy to return to his parents.

"Take one and bite down hard." Hanako pointed to the pile of sticks at Kenji's feet.

With a sigh, Kenji once again did as he was told and placed a stick between his teeth.

"Now this will not feel very good, but you cannot whine about it okay?"

Kenji rolled his eyes as he tried to ignore the taste of the stick in his mouth.

"Okay, here you go." Hanako opened her hand to allow the maggots to find their way to Kenji's wound.

The stick snapped as Kenji arched his back and let out a groan. Every muscle felt like it was contracting as the maggots began to gnaw off the dead and dirty skin lining his cut.

"That's it, you're doing great." Hanako gave Kenji a pat on the head as she did the boy.

Kenji gave the rock a hard smack with his left fist as he felt the sensation of maggots crawling across his now raw skin. Keeping his fist clenched he drove it into the ground as the maggots continued to eat.

"There, see, it's not so bad, we just have to leave them there to do their work," Hanako said calmly.

"If it's not so bad, then you try it."

Hanako giggled as she ripped a piece off the bottom of her dress and began to place it over the cut to hold the maggots in place. She followed up by rolling up another piece into a long cylinder and wrapping it around the first to hold it in place. She finished by tying the ends of the second piece together and sat back to admire her work.

"It's not pretty, but it should hold together."

"Should?"

"It will, you big baby, and what about a thank you?"

"I'm sorry, you're right. I appreciate this."

"Well, you're welcome. Now should we tell everyone to get to bed?"

"Why we? They know you."

"But they trust you. You saved us."

"But what if their trust is misplaced?"

"Is it?"

Kenji shrugged.

"Look, these people have been through a lot already. But they'll listen to you because you helped get them here. That's all the trust they need. We'll talk to them together."

"Fine, let's go."

The pair stood up to address the group. Hanako began by raising her arms above her head to help her gain everyone's attention.

"Okay everyone. I know we have all had a long day and there are a lot of different emotions running through the group right now, but before we call it a night Kenji has a few things to say." She stepped back to let Kenji speak.

"Hello everyone, I'm Kenji. There are a few things I would like to go over before we go to sleep."

What are you a school teacher? Get on with it already. Kenji thought to himself.

"First off we are going to be finding a spot to sleep in the cave tonight. It will fit everyone but I think we should give choice of spots to women and children first."

Kenji paused as the group looked around and collectively nodded at the suggestion.

"Next, each night we should have someone on watch and we can have some volunteers rotate out so we can stay as rested and as safe as we can. You have all had a long day today so for tonight I'll stay up to watch for you."

Once again, the group nodded, and Kenji noticed Hanako's mother give a smile.

"In the morning, we can discuss more about what our next plans are but for now we should all get some sleep. I know it's been hard but we are here together now and we will be here together in the morning."

Kenji glanced at Hanako who was smiling back at him.

"Okay, let's get some sleep everyone."

The group stumbled to their feet and made their way to the entrance of the cave. Hanako and her mother began guiding people inside and making sure they could find a spot on the cave floor. As the group walked past Kenji he was met with more smiles and a few hands were placed on his shoulder as they passed him. Kenji looked at the ground as the last of the group made their way inside.

"You did good Kenji, they're thankful." Kenji looked up to see Hanako's mother staring back at him. Kenji nodded.

"Thanks."

Hanako's mother stepped inside the cave followed by Hanako as Kenji picked up the first bundle of branches and leaves to cover the entrance.

"Now you make sure you're still there in the morning." Hanako said to Kenji as she sat down inside.

"I'll do my best." Kenji smiled back as he placed the first batch of branches.

As Kenji put down the final set of branches against the cave entrance, he took a deep breath in and closed his eyes to exhale. Turning around he opened them to face the forest and walked out to the edge of the clearing. Putting his hand out to steady himself against the trunk of a tree Kenji peered out into the forest as if trying to see all the way back to Sekigahara. He wondered how long it would take Tokugawa's men to find him out here. As he stared back into the darkness of the forest Kenji's arm was nudged off the tree causing him to stumble. He turned to face Strider who had come to accompany him.

"How do you do it?" Kenji asked. Strider's deep black eyes staring back at him.

"You have seen so much war, so much death. How do you cope with it all?"

Strider craned his head from side to side as a fly buzzed to close to his space.

"Or maybe you don't. Is that it? You don't cope with it; you just learn to live with it."

Strider gave a small neigh and trotted off having been fed up with the fly.

"Well, good talk."

Kenji looked back toward the forest as the day's events spiraled through his mind. Everything had happened so quickly it was almost too hard to process all at once.

Suddenly Kenji looked up as the trees in front of him burst into flames and the fire rose to engulf the canopy above him. Kenji spun quickly looking for some way to stop the fire from spreading but as he turned again to face the inferno it had stopped. As quickly as it had started the fire was snuffed out and Kenji was left once again staring into the darkness ahead of him.

What was that? Kenji tried to make sense of what he had just seen.

His thoughts were interrupted however by the sharp snap of a twig and as his eyes turned to meet the sudden sound, Kenji unsheathed his sword and held it out at his own neck height stopping as he felt the blade hit its mark. Kenji's sharp gaze was met by the terrified eyes of Maku, a single drop of blood dripping down his neck.

"Well hello to you too." Maku said, careful not to breathe too heavy lest his neck get pushed any farther against Kenji's blade.

"Kenji, I know what you might be thinking but please let me explain."

Kenji's eyes darted from side to side looking out at the forest around them, his sword not dropping from Maku's neck.

"Kenji I wasn't followed, I promise. To be honest I didn't even know that I would run into you out here. You're probably just as surprised as I am."

"Why are you here?" Kenji's eyes were again focused on Maku.

"I ran Kenji, after the fighting. I'm not sure if anyone even knows that I'm alive except for you."

Kenji lowered his sword and turned to face his friend.

"And you said you weren't followed?"

"No, I promise. Why are you out here?"

"It's kind of a long story." Kenji sheathed his sword.

"I guess I have time now."

The pair sat down in the grass and Maku leaned back on his hands.

"We took the city, but at great cost. I thought I had lost you in the fighting."

"I thought that was the case, but after I killed the man who attacked me, I lost sight of you. Before I knew it, everything went dark. I must have been knocked out because when I woke up, I had the corpse of a soldier on top of me and my ears were ringing."

"Why didn't you go to the city?"

"I didn't know who had won. I could have been walking into an enemy city. There was no one around me anymore so, I ran." Maku looked down at the grass. "I didn't know what else to do."

"I ran too. After we entered the city Tokugawa's men starting pillaging it, killing women and children."

Maku looked back up, his eyes wide.

"I disagreed with it so I stood up to Tokugawa and he tried to kill me. I thought it was all over right then but..." Kenji paused. "My uncle got in the way of his blade."

"Oh Kenji, I'm really sorry." Maku put his hand on Kenji's shoulder.

"There are others you know."

"Others?" A look of confusion crossed over Maku's face.

"In the cave behind us, there are other survivors from the city. They're asleep right now. I'm protecting them."

"But why? That is not your responsibility."

"Maku we took everything from them. They were innocent in all of this and we took their whole lives away from them."

"Of course, you're right. I'm sorry. So, what do we do now?"

"Well, I told them I would keep watch for tonight and in the morning we will come up with a plan."

"But what happens when they see me? I don't think they will take too kindly to me in this armour."

"I'll tell them you're with me. They seem to trust me."

"I guess if you're sure."

Kenji leaned back on his hands to match Maku.

"And besides, if they don't like you, you have already had ample practice running away."

"Hey!" Maku pushed Kenji.

"What? It's true. In the morning maybe you could race the horse back to Sekigahara, give the folks a good show." Kenji said with a grin.

"Hey that's not funny."

"Come on, it's a little funny."

"Fine I'll do it, but only if you carry me back afterwards." Maku said with a chuckle.

"Ha, maybe I will." Kenji laughed.

This sparked laughter between the pair and they continued to laugh into the night as the light from the moon began to creep its way onto the forest floor.

CHAPTER 12

"Uncle, Uncle no not now... Uncle!"

"Wha-!" Kenji sat straight up and unsheathed his sword aiming it at an unknown foe.

"Woah hey, Kenji it's just me. No one else is here." Maku was standing looking out at the forest.

"The people are still in the cave, none ever came out. They're probably still asleep."

Kenji put his sword on his back and stood up. The sun was beginning to creep through the tree line and into the clearing.

"Okay, thank you. How long was I out?"

"For most of the night. Nothing happened though. The forest was quiet."

"Sorry, it will not happen again."

"No no, don't worry about it. You needed the sleep."

"Yes, I guess I did. So, no one has come out yet?"

"Nope. Must all still be sleeping."

"Okay, that's fine."

"So, what do we do? Do we have food here?"

"No. We'll need to go out for some."

"Well I have my bow, we can use that, right?"

"Oh yes, yes we can." Kenji looked at Maku's back, noticing for the first time the bow slung over his shoulder.

How did I not notice yesterday? I really must have been tired.

The pair stood up and faced the forest. Kenji looked back at the cave as if trying to see signs of motion through the rock face.

"Don't worry Kenji. We'll be back before any of them are up."

"Yes."

Kenji led Maku into the forest. The woods were dark and thick, the sun still too low to be able to make its way through the trees.

"So you've gone hunting with that bow before?" Kenji asked, pushing his way through some thick brush.

"Yes, a couple of times. I would sometimes be picked to be part of the hunting party when the army was on the move."

"I'll let you take the shot then."

"Do you know how to track? I was never very good at that part."

"Yes, I'll find us the animal as long as you will not miss."

"Will do."

The pair moved through the forest, Maku's eyes fixed on the trees ahead of them. Kenji's eyes did not follow Maku's gaze but were surveying the ground instead. He scanned the area just ahead of their feet looking for any signs of wildlife that had recently travelled the path they now walked. Kenji started hearing sounds around him and realized it was not the wildlife but his friend walked adjacent to him. Whether he meant to or not, Maku rustled the leaves and underbrush beneath their feet. Kenji was careful not to make that mistake when trying to stay quiet, another trick his uncle had taught him. Not allowing his mind to drift Kenji spotted a patch of grass that stood out.

"Here." Kenji stopped and knelt down to have a closer look at what caught his eye.

"What is it? Something we can track?"

"I think so yes. Look here."

Kenji pointed to a section of the grass that was flatter than the blades surrounding it. The blades of grass were pushed down in an oval shape on the ground.

"What does it mean?" Maku looked at the spot of grass hoping to learn from his friend.

"That we could be close. By the size of it I would say it's a fairly large animal." Kenji traced the outline with his finger.

"It was probably resting here for a time. And look..." Kenji's eyes darted to a new point of interest. Maku's followed in anticipation.

"See the grass and weeds there? They're bent to the side which probably means the animal got up and left in a hurry causing the plants to bend sideways as it ran through them."

"So how do we find it?"

"Follow the path it left for us. See how you can see the same pattern running in a line out into the forest?"

"Oh yes." Maku traced the line of angled weeds and undergrowth into the forest with his eyes. "But it could be long gone by now."

Kenji's voice switched to a hushed tone.

"Not necessarily." Kenji's eyes were locked onto another new target. "Stay low and look past that tree."

Maku crouched and readied to lower his voice to match Kenji's.

"Now look into the bush on the right side of the trunk. Do you see?"

Maku peered hard into the depth of the forest.

"What is it? I see a brown patch and white spots?"

"Nihonjika. Deer."

"What is it doing? It's just lying there."

The deer was lying just behind the bush, its stomach sprawled on the forest floor.

"It must have noticed us approach."

"Then why didn't it keep running?"

"Nihonjika tend to sprawl when sensing a hunter nearby. I don't think it knows we can see it."

The deer's head was low to the ground, it's breathing slow and controlled.

"Should I take the shot?"

"Can you hit it from here?"

"I bet I can."

"Then go ahead. I'll call it to see if I can get it to raise its head. But remember if you miss, we could lose it for good." Kenji paused. "And all the people back at the cave will go hungry."

"Thanks for that." Maku took his bow off his back and notched an arrow.

"Anytime."

Maku stood just enough so he could hold his bow vertically. Kenji sat back in the grass and watched Maku prepare for the shot. His breathing slowed and he cocked his right elbow up to be in line with his shoulder. As he drew the arrow back the string tightened and he took a breath in. Kenji gave a sharp whistle and the deer's head craned up looking for the noise. At the same moment, Maku exhaled and loosed the arrow, and a panicked cry could be heard from the bush. The deer got up and stumbled a few steps before falling back over behind the trunk of the tree.

"Nice shot." Kenji complimented his friend as he stood up.

"Thanks." Maku smiled and slung his bow back over his shoulder.

"Let's go get it."

The duo walked over to the animal that was knocked down a couple of feet from where it was before. Kenji knelt down next to the animal as if to inspect it.

"Male, and still fairly young by the looks of it."

The deer's breathing was short and quick. The arrow was pierced into its neck just above its shoulder. A small collection of blood was surrounding the point of injury. Kenji took a breath in and put his hand on the animal's shoulder just below where the arrow had entered.

"You'll help a lot of people." Kenji spoke to the animal.

He unsheathed his sword and inserted it just above the arrow. One final huff of air was exerted from the animal as its head fell to the grass. Kenji grasped the arrow by its shaft and pulled it out letting more trapped blood escape from the now open hole. He stood and handed the still intact arrow back to Maku who wiped it off on his pants before placing it back in his quiver.

"I'll carry it back to camp. The sun will be up soon."

Kenji crouched again beside the body and slid his hands underneath its stomach. Lifting with his knees he hoisted the carcass up in front of his chest. His right arm suddenly filled with heat and he held his breath not wanting to show that his shoulder was not healed enough to carry the body without any pain to go with the action. Maku still noticed.

"You alright pal?"

"Oh yes, it's just my shoulder."

"I can carry it if you need." Maku offered.

"No, no, it's only back to camp."

"Ha, show off."

Kenji smirked as he lowered his head and hoisted the deer onto his shoulders, shifting his grips to hold the animal's legs on either side of his face.

The pair arrived at camp to find Hanako and some of the parents and children up and about. The kids were splashing around in the pond, laughing when water sprayed their smiles. A couple people were gathering sticks and placing them down next to the cave. Hanako was talking to one of the mothers and nodded when Kenji and Maku approached from the treeline. Kenji dropped the deer at the women's feet and the women gave a slightly disgusted look back to the pair. Kenji responded with a big grin.

"Ewww..." One of the children called out from the pond.

"That'll keep us fed." Hanako said, waving to the woman who went off to play with the children.

"That's the idea." Kenji replied.

Hanako shifted her gaze to Maku and her eyes narrowed as she noticed the armour he wore.

"Hanako this is Maku, he fought with me." Maku nodded his head in greeting. "He's not a danger, don't worry."

"Alright, hopefully he can keep you in line." She said with a grin.

Kenji rolled his eyes and looked over at Maku.

"See, its fine, as long as you can deal with being around her."

"I think I'll be alright." Maku looked down at the deer that lay at the groups' feet. "Should I get a fire going?"

"I think that's a good idea." Hanako said. "The people here are dying to eat."

"I'll take my leave then, pleasure to meet you Hanako."

"Same to you."

Maku grabbed the deer's legs and began dragging it toward the cave.

"How's the group doing?" Kenji asked, looking back at Hanako now.

"Alright I think. The kids don't seem too bothered just yet but that's to be expected. Most of us are up and about but some are still sleeping."

"Well, it was a long day yesterday."

"Yes, it was. There has been talk about what to do next; some have suggested hiding here a while longer. Some want to leave."

"Once everyone is up we can discuss what the right thing to do is."

"But Kenji what is the right thing? We don't really have anywhere to go."

"I know. I wish I knew what to do next but our priority will be the group as a whole. Figuring out what we need for ourselves first."

"The food was a start. Could you and Maku teach others how to do that?"

Kenji looked around at the people who were already up, a handful of kids and some of the parents. He guessed most had never hunted before.

"I'm sure we could try, but we only have the one bow."

"Can we learn how to make traps?"

"With what materials? We have no weapons or tools."

"Yes, you're right. I can talk to some of the others and see what everyone brought with them."

"Alright, that's a start. Let me know when everyone is up and we can gather together and talk about a plan."

"Alright, what will you do now?"

"I'm going to go help Maku with the deer and maybe meet some of the others more formally."

"Okay, I'll come get you once everyone is up."

"Sounds good."

Kenji and Hanako parted ways both off to work on their separate tasks. Kenji walked over to Maku who was already finishing with the deer's pelt. He had set up a small circle of rocks and placed some wood in the centre preparing for the fire. The deer was off to one side, most of its hide already removed. As Kenji approached, Maku was cutting off the last of the deer's hide and had begun rolling it up beside him.

"You made quick work of that deer." Kenji said taking a knee down beside his friend.

"I have had some practice." Maku said wiping off his blade on his pant leg.

"Do you need any help?"

"No, I should be fine. The hard part is finished, I'm just going to try and portion it as best I can."

"Perfect. Once everyone is up we are going to gather and talk about our plan." Kenji said standing back up now.

"Do we have one?" Maku asked looking up at Kenji.

"Well, not really, but I was going to leave that out of the talk."

"That's probably for the best."

"I was talking with Hanako about our supplies. If we are going to survive out here, we are going to need tools and weapons. Right now we are the only two with any weapons. The others didn't look like they had time to grab much else."

"Well, I don't see any shops around here."

"No, me either and that's our problem. I'll keep thinking on it."

"Alright, I need to finish up with this deer."

"No problem, I'll leave you to it. Thanks, Maku."

"You're welcome."

Kenji left with a wave and made his way to the centre of the clearing to watch the activities of the morning. He knew he should probably get to know the others sooner than later. But where to start? Before he had much time to decide he was greeted by the woman whose daughter he had saved in the escape. She looked not much older than Hanako but had long black hair partially covering one side of her face. As she approached, she brushed her hair over her ear to reveal what was covered.

"I'm Cho. We were never properly introduced and I never got the chance to truly thank you for what you did for me and my daughter."

"Don't mention it; it was the right thing to do."

"Well you're very kind. Aiko will not stop talking about you."

"She's doing alright after all this?"

"I'm not so sure she really understands everything just yet. Maybe that's for the best. She seems happy with the other children." Cho glanced toward the pond full of children.

"I'm sorry again about your husband." Kenji said sharing a glance toward the water.

"Thank you. I'm just hoping I can find a way to explain it to Aiko."

"Well, if you need anything let me know. We are going to gather once the deer is prepared and everyone is up to decide on the next step."

"Okay, I should go check on Aiko. It was nice to talk with you."

Kenji nodded. "And you as well."

Kenji watched as Cho met with her daughter and picked her up in her arms. Aiko began to laugh as she was spun around in her mother's arms. This caused the kids to form a line in front of Cho all wanting a turn to be spun around. Kenji smiled as he watched every kid one by one get a turn with Cho, each one enjoying it as much as the last. Kenji wished the same mood could infuse the whole group but he was not so sure. He continued to survey the group. Adding Maku, the group was now eighteen people. A sizeable group to take care of, but that also meant lots of people to get many different tasks done. was something to talk about once everyone was up.

"Excuse me son, may have a word with you?"

Kenji turned his head as he was approached by an older man who, despite his age, seemed to move with ease toward him.

"Of course, yes. What do you need? Is everything alright?"

"Oh yes. Well, as alright as things can be, I suppose. I'm Saburo." The older man presented his hand to Kenji.

"It's a pleasure to meet you sir, I'm Kenji." He shook hands with him.

"I heard we needed tools for the group if we are going to do well out here. I thought I might offer a suggestion."

"What did you have in mind?" Kenji asked, now slightly intrigued.

"Back in the city I was a wood worker you see, and I could help construct some things for us here."

"That would be very helpful sir."

"Yes, but the problem is, all my notes and tools were left in my shop in the city and I don't really have any desire to go back there right now."

"I can understand that."

"If you could find a way back in, I could give you my key, and hopefully you could retrieve my items for me."

"That comes with a lot of risks."

"Yes, it does. But I had heard this rumour going around you have already made this type of trip once before."

Kenji stopped to think how that story had already begun to be told. He thought Hanako might have let it slip.

"Do you have the key with you?"

"Of course, I always keep in on my person. The shop is mine and mine alone. I planned on passing it on to my son Naoko."

"We will be getting together soon to talk about what to do next. I can bring that up with everyone."

"Very good."

"If I may sir, you don't seem to terribly bothered by our circumstances here."

"What's done is done. And I can do nothing to change what has happened. I can only hope to offer help and to look forward."

"That's a very good attitude to have sir."

"Please my boy, call me Saburo."

"Well Saburo, you've been very helpful, thank you. I'll bring it up with the rest of the group."

"Excellent. I am going to check on my wife, I would not want her worrying about me leaving the cave without her."

Saburo turned and began walking back toward the cave.

"No, we would not. It was nice meeting you Saburo."

"You as well Kenji." Saburo called back over his shoulder.

Kenji began to ponder the idea of staying here long term. It was not something he had considered or even thought feasible. Then again, this was never a scenario he had ever thought about. He was so used to keeping on the move when he was with Ichiro, the two of them never really stayed in one place for very long. But with a group this size he knew it would prove much more difficult to cover lots of ground, especially with only the one horse. Kenji looked over to Strider who was content with grazing from the grass around him. He liked Strider, but was undecided on whether it was right to keep him around. He knew how helpful it would be to have a horse but Strider had already dealt with so much war, and he wondered if it would be fairer just to let him go. For now, Strider would stay.

Kenji continued to think as he walked over to Maku, who had gotten a fire started and was cooking the venison for the group. Chunks of meat were already prepared and were placed on some flatter stones around Maku.

"Sorry, those were the best plates I could find." Maku said without looking up from the fire.

"That's just fine Maku, as long as you cooked the meat all the way through," Kenji said, giving Maku a little kick.

"Don't worry Kenji, I will not kill anyone."

"Perfect. I was talking to Saburo, one of the group members, and he came up with a plan to get us some tools. But it's a little risky."

"What did he say?"

"Well, it involves going back into the city."

"Oh yes? And who in this group is going to willingly volunteer for exactly?"

"That's the trouble. I'm going to bring it up with the others but I want you to stay here. Someone needs to watch over this place."

"I can do that, but good luck with finding some help on this. I…"

"Sorry to interrupt boys, but everyone is up now and there are a lot of questions already." Hanako had arrived behind Kenji.

"Alright, I'll be there in just a moment."

"Okay, and make sure to bring the food." Hanako left to join the others once more.

"I'll go talk with the group. See if we can come up with some jobs for everyone."

"Agreed. I'll be there right away, I'm almost finished with this."

"Alright."

Kenji turned and walked to the group, who had begun seating themselves in a circle in the center of the clearing. Some had begun to pull logs over to sit on while others were getting comfortable in the grass. Kenji stood on the outside of the circle of people with Hanako and her mother seated in front of him on the grass. Across from him were Saburo and his wife seated on one of the logs and their son standing behind them. Cho came to sit beside Hanako and they greeted each other with a smile. The rest of the group, whom Kenji had yet to meet, placed themselves down and tried to get comfortable, while the kids continued to play in the grass. Kenji looked around the circle, wondering who was going to be the first to speak or if he had to. Luckily, he did not have to decide because Hanako began the conversation.

"Alright everyone, I hope you all slept as well as you could. There are some things we need to discuss and I hope to address all of it. But if there is something you want to say the floor is open."

Hanako patiently waited to see if there was anything the others wanted to bring up.

"Very well. First off I know we are all hungry but thanks to Kenji and his friend Maku they have brought us back a deer and it should be ready in a few moments."

"Are you sure he didn't poison it?" Someone from the group spoke up.

"I assure you, you have nothing to worry about with Maku. I trust him and I ask you do the same." Kenji said scanning to see who it was who brought it up.

Cho turned to face Kenji.

"I'm sorry Kenji, but that might take us some time."

"Cho don't worry, you can take the time but no one has anything to fear." Hanako said trying to reassure the group.

Kenji stepped up to speak again.

"I would like to help teach those willing to hunt, that way we have an easier time staying fed. The main problem is, we don't have enough equipment for everyone to use."

"And that's why we came up with a plan," said Saburo.

"That's right. It's risky, but hear me out."

"Should we really be taking risks right now?" One of the men asked Kenji.

He was a younger man with short black hair and a stocky frame, sitting with his wife and son beside Saburo and his family.

"Kane, let's hear him out. I'm sure he has thought it through." This time Hanako's mother interjected.

Kane's shoulders slumped but he fell silent to let Kenji finish.

"Saburo told me he was a wood worker in the city and his shop could have the items we need to start surviving out here."

"Are you suggesting we go back there?" A woman piped up.

"You must be nuts." Another man said.

Kenji put his hands in the air to try and calm the crowd.

"Look, all I'm asking for is two volunteers to come with me. I believe I know a way to get in without being noticed, but I need someone to watch my back."

"Let me go with you." Saburo's son spoke out. "I know my way around my father's shop. I could get you in and out quicker."

Kenji looked to Saburo who gave his nod of approval back.

"Alright. Anyone else?"

The group was silent again, some refusing to look up from the ground.

"I'll go too." A man stood up from his wife who shot him a slightly angry look.

"Good, thank you. I'm going to leave at sundown. We can talk more about the plan then."

At that moment, Maku began to arrive with arms full of rocks carrying slabs of meat on top.

"I know it might not look it but it will taste fine. I promise." Maku began passing out the food.

"Thank you Maku." Kenji nodded to his friend. "While you eat, I'll talk about the other thought I had."

The group was too busy hurriedly eating the deer they had been served to interject.

"We can decide amongst ourselves who should do what, but we should split off some tasks to pairs or groups, such as gathering materials from the forest or more firewood."

"When we were living in the city, I studied local plants. I could show which berries are safe to eat around here." The woman sitting beside Kane said in between bites.

"Yes, perfect. Thank you." Kenji smiled. "Lastly we should start to set up rotations of people to stay up for watch overnight. We can make sure to switch out every couple of hours so we can all get rest."

Kenji paused.

"Any questions?"

The group paid Kenji little attention now that they had food in front of them.

"Very well, those of you who are coming with me tonight come see me once you are done eating."

A few of the members of the group nodded as Kenji turned to leave but most just continued to eat.

"Here Kenji I made sure to save you some." Maku handed Kenji a flat rock with more of the deer on top.

"Thanks, Maku. Let's eat."

"Agreed."

The pair walked over to the edge of the pond and took a seat next to one another. Kenji took a long breath in as he sat down, enjoying the misty breeze from the pond brush over his face. The clearing was quiet and serene, the only noise coming from hushed conversation from the other members of the group. Kenji was unsure whether they were trying to stay quiet to avoid possible soldiers passing by or just not wanting him to hear them, but either way it did not bother him. He had only met a few of them so far and it would take time for everyone to talk openly to him. But he did not mind, he had Maku and Hanako to talk to, and for right now that was all he needed. As he ate, Kenji's thoughts became fixated on the city. He did not entirely agree with the plan, and was concerned about putting others in danger, but he could not think of a better way to get tools. He closed his eyes and tried to envision the route he would take to enter the city, but the only thing he could see was the courtyard. Tokugawa was standing there in front of him sword drawn. All Kenji could do was stand there and wait for the strike he knew was coming. Tokugawa lunged forward, sword aimed right for Kenji's stomach. Then Kenji's eyes shot open once again. Kenji turned to look at Maku who was busy eating beside him.

"Mind if I join you?" Hanako approached the boys from the group in middle of the clearing.

"Sure." Maku said with a full mouth.

Hanako took a spot on the other side of Maku and sat with her hands in her lap. She had already finished her food.

"So, what's the story with you two?"

"What do you mean?" Kenji asked.

"I mean, why are you together in this? You seem to trust each other."

"Trust is built when you fight beside someone." Kenji said, swallowing the last of his food.

"Not to mention he saved my life." Maku responded.

"We saved each other's lives." Kenji countered.

"Well, I'm glad to have you two around. I don't think there is anyone else here who would be able to defend the group if it came down to it."

"I'm sure they would not go down without a fight." Kenji said as he tossed his rock away into the pond.

"Well it would be a really short fight." Hanako said, with amusement in her voice.

"Maybe we could help with that." Maku suggested. "We could teach them how to fight."

"Perhaps, but I'm not sure everyone would be up for it."

"Regardless, we don't have the equipment to train them with. We'll need to get into the city first." Kenji said.

"And you're sure you want me to stay here? I could watch your back."

"Maku, I need someone back to defend the camp and you're the only other person here with a weapon."

Maku's shoulders slumped.

"Yes, you're right."

"So, who are the two going with me?" Kenji turned his attention to Hanako now.

"You already met Saburo, it's his son Naoko. As long as I have known him, he has been trying to live up to his father. Saburo is a very skilled woodworker and has been preparing Naoko to take his shop. I guess will not happen now." Hanako looked to the grass.

"And the other man? His wife didn't seem too happy he volunteered."

"I don't know Jiro well, but I know he has worked really hard to be with his wife Riku. I heard he had a crush on her for the longest time."

"How did he win her over?" Maku asked.

"From the story I heard, he challenged one of the guards in town to an arm wrestle to show her how strong he was."

"Wow." Kenji rolled his eyes.

"I think it was cute." Hanako protested.

"Will he actually be a help when I bring him along then?"

"I think so, yes. He seems like the type who works hard for recognition."

"As long as he doesn't go too far to achieve it."

"I'm sure you'll be fine."

"I better go gather my things before sundown. We'll make sure to come back with supplies." Kenji got up to leave.

"And in one piece." Hanako added.

"Right, that too."

Kenji began to walk toward Strider who had been carrying most of his equipment. Kenji had his swords with him at almost all times but he left his satchel, rope and cleaning cloth with Strider. As he approached, Strider neighed and trotted in a small circle. Kenji put his hand on the horse's neck and gave him a pat, letting him know he only needed supplies from him. As if he was sad he was not being taken for a ride, Strider bowed his head and waited patiently as Kenji retrieved his things from the saddle. He hooked the rope to his belt and slung the satchel over his shoulder, and put his cloth inside. Kenji thanked Strider by rubbing his neck before leaving to go and find his companions for the trip. The sun was still shining above the canopy of the forest but Kenji wanted to make sure he went through the plan well in advance. First, he needed to find Saburo to retrieve the key to his shop.

CHAPTER 13

Saburo was busy talking with his son Naoko as Kenji arrived. Not wanting to intrude, Kenji stood to the side as the pair discussed something out of his earshot. As Saburo was talking, he noticed Kenji over his son's shoulder and gave a slight nod as if to say "just one moment." Kenji folded his hands in front of him and waited patiently for the conversation to cease. After giving his son a pat on the shoulder Saburo waved Kenji into the conversation.

"My son and I were just talking about my shop. I made sure he remembered where I had everything stashed away."

"Very good, you are still okay to come with me?" Kenji asked.

"Yes, I know where everything is. We should be in and out very quickly."

"Excellent. I don't want to spend any more time there than we have to."

"Agreed."

Kenji turned his attention back to Saburo now.

"You mentioned you have the key with you? I should take it now."

"With all due respect son, I would like Naoko to hold on to the key. It is a family business."

Kenji did not feel the need to argue that point.

"Very well, I should still come inside with you though to watch your back."

"Yes, of course." Naoko replied.

"Have either of you seen Jiro? He is the other part of our party."

"I believe I saw him talking to his wife by the entrance to the cave," Saburo said, lifting a finger to point at the cave.

"Good. Naoko are you all set to go?"

"Yes, I think I am."

"Perfect, would you mind waiting by the edge of the clearing. I'll go and get Jiro."

"Sure thing."

Naoko left toward the edge of camp as Kenji began to go and get the other member of their party before feeling a firm hand on his shoulder.

"Kenji, make sure you bring my boy back in one piece, will you?" Saburo said with a solemn look in his eyes.

"Of course, Saburo, I'll make sure nothing happens to him."

Saburo released Kenji's shoulder letting his hand drop back to his side.

"Very well, good luck."

"Thank you."

Kenji turned again to begin walking toward Jiro but this time began to contemplate the different possible outcomes of this trip. The only one he wanted to think about was the ending where they all were returned safely.

As Kenji approached Jiro he was having his own conversation with his wife but immediately invited Kenji to join in their group.

"Ah Kenji, it was Kenji, right? I'm Jiro and this is my lovely wife Riku." Jiro outstretched his arm in front of Riku as if to put his wife on display.

"It's a pleasure to meet you both."

"So, are we leaving on this adventure of ours?"

"That was the plan. I have Naoko waiting by the treeline. I was just coming to see if you were ready."

"Yes, I believe I am but much to the disappointment of my wife I'm afraid."

"Ma'am, I promise all of us, including your husband, will return safely. I'll see to it that we do."

Riku gave Kenji a slight nod giving her approval but refrained from saying a word.

"Alright should we get going then?" Jiro asked showing his obvious eagerness to leave.

"Yes, we can, follow me."

Jiro turned to kiss his wife on the head before the pair left to meet up with Naoko at the edge of camp.

"Do you think there will be lots of guards when we get there?" Jiro asked.

"The plan is to avoid them as much as possible."

"If we do see some, you'll deal with them, right? I mean, I would but you seem to be better suited to it than I."

"That's the idea." Kenji answered, starting to wish he hadn't asked for volunteers.

The two men met up with Naoko as he was embracing his mother who was smiling, but the kind of smile that was hiding worry underneath. She nodded as the two men approached and left to go join the rest of the camp once again.

"We're all set?" Naoko asked.

"Yes, we are. It's alright if we discuss the plan on the way? I'm hoping to cover lots of ground before nightfall."

"You're the boss." Jiro replied.

"Okay, let's get to it."

Kenji noticed a wave from Hanako who was standing by the edge of the pond and he responded with a wave of his own before leading the trio into the forest.

The sun had become low enough to create shadows across the bed of the forest as the trio made their way deeper in the woods. Kenji surveyed the space around them, wary of any possible patrols they might encounter. He made sure to walk with his heel landing first then rolling onto the ball of his foot, working to make his steps as quiet as possible. His partners were clearly not working as hard at it.

"I was thinking I'll use the rope in my bag to get us to the top of the wall while Jiro you keep watch."

"I can definitely do that. What should I do after?"

"I want you to catch the rope as I toss it back to you and retreat to the cover of the trees so we don't alert any of the archers on the wall."

"Got it. I'll be as quick as a deer." Jiro responded with confidence.

"Great. Naoko you still have the key to your father's shop?"

"Yes, right here." Naoko opened a piece of folded cloth to display a small metal key placed inside.

"Good. I'll scale the wall and make sure it is safe for you to come up then you can follow. But don't come up unless I give you the signal."

"Right."

"Once over it will be your job to lead us to your father's shop and I'll watch your back as you grab the equipment."

A rustle in the leaves next to them caused the group to stop in their tracks and Kenji turned to face the noise, his arm already cocked back to grasp his sword. He let out a sigh as a small blackbird flew out of the branches and out over the group's head.

"Come on, we're nearly there now." Kenji motioned for the group to continue onward.

As they walked, Kenji's mind drifted back to the courtyard. He could see the bricks lining the ground at his feet. He saw the wide doors to the royal house slide open as Tokugawa stepped through them now in place of Mitsunari. He shook his head and focused on the task at hand. The darkening sky made it hard to make it out, but Kenji could now see the bottom of the wall as they approached the edge of the forest. He lowered his stance as he approached the trunk of a nearby tree and motioned for the others to do the same, then turned to speak in a hushed tone.

"Alright, remember the plan?"

Jiro and Naoko nodded in unison.

"Good, Naoko follow me when I give the signal."

Kenji reached into his satchel as he surveyed the wall looking for any archers that might occupy it. Knotting the end of the rope to create a loop at the end he watched as an archer patrolled past the top of the wall. Waiting for the soldier to move a good distance away Kenji began to swing the rope at his side aiming for the top of the wall. Throwing the end of the rope toward the wall he watched as the loop snagged at the top and he gave a pull to ensure it was secure.

"Get ready to stay close behind me." Kenji said back to Naoko.

Kenji stood and began running up toward the base of the wall, rope in hand. As he gained speed he jumped up toward the wall and gripping the rope tightly he planted both feet firmly against it. As he scaled the wall Kenji watched for the archer who had yet to return back his way. Once atop the wall, Kenji knelt down and waved for Naoko to join him. Naoko tried to copy Kenji's climb but was breathing heavily halfway to the top. Clearly, he had done nothing like this before. Kenji threw down his hand to help Naoko conquer the top of the wall and began to unhook the rope from the top. Looking quickly to make sure they had not been seen, Kenji tossed the rope back to the ground where a scurrying Jiro came to pick it up before returning to the cover of the trees. Giving Jiro a wave before turning around, Kenji set his sights on the safest way to get both he and Naoko to the ground. He began to run low across the top of the wall with Naoko close behind him. Once the pair made it to a rooftop close to the edge of the wall, Kenji stopped to turn to his partner.

"Ready?"

"I'll follow your lead."

Kenji turned back to the rooftop and leapt on to it from above. Landing safely on his feet, he pivoted back around to watch over Naoko. After slight hesitation Naoko followed Kenji and jumped onto the roof to join him but upon his landing his foot slipped causing him to put his arms out to soften the blow.

"You good?"

"Yes, I'll just be sore tomorrow." Naoko responded rubbing his forearms.

"Which way is best?"

"My father's shop is down this way." Naoko said pointing behind Kenji to a stretch of buildings adjacent to the one they were currently on top of.

"Down this way then." Kenji said crawling to the edge of the rooftop.

Kenji surveyed the alley behind the building before jumping down into the street. He turned and watched Naoko do the same.

"Wait, up against the wall!" Kenji pinned himself to the wall which caused Naoko to do the same.

"The guard is walking above us." Kenji pointed a single finger skyward at the archer who had made his way back to them.

Kenji raised his finger to his lips as the guard patrolled above the pair. Naoko's eyes went wide as they listened to the sound of the man's boots hit the stone over their heads. Kenji pointed to the wall and then down the alley, telling Naoko it was time to move. The duo moved along the wall a few feet behind the patrolling guard until Kenji felt a tap on his shoulder. Naoko had stopped and was motioning toward the building next to them.

"Here?" Kenji whispered.

Naoko nodded.

"Door?"

Again, Naoko nodded and got out the key he had been carrying.

"I'll watch." Kenji said as Naoko knelt down by the back door to the shop.

Kenji surveyed both the top of the wall and the alley they were in for any more patrols that might cause them trouble. Kenji's head turned again as he heard the click of the lock telling him it was time to go.

Naoko and Kenji entered the woodshop and Kenji closed the door behind them making sure to not let it hit its frame too hard. The shop was a modest size, with the back entrance giving way to a mostly open main floor filled with shelves stocked with wooden boards and other building materials. The counter in the center of the floor had shelves carved into the back which Naoko began searching. Kenji walked past the counter to a set of stairs leading to a second level of the shop.

"That was our bedroom." Naoko whispered. "See if you can find a journal up there."

Kenji made his way up the staircase and into a smaller room comprised of two beds and a few pieces of furniture. To the side of one bed was a small nightstand which caught Kenji's eye. He walked over and opened the top drawer to find a small red journal as the sole occupant. Kenji took the journal and stuffed it into his satchel before turning to leave and join Naoko on the main floor. As he moved back to the staircase, the light from the moon caused a glint to appear off objects lying in the corner. As Kenji walked closer, he was surprised to see half a dozen swords on the floor. Each had its own cover and rope allowing Kenji to fit two more over his shoulder and carry the last four down the stairs. As he came down, Kenji shot a confused look toward Naoko who had a small wooden box in his hands.

"Oh right, my father was sometimes asked to make the handles for the soldiers' weapons. Those must have been left here before being handed out. Lucky no one has searched here yet."

"Can you carry any?" Kenji extended his arms out toward Naoko.

"Sure. What about this box though?"

"What's in it?"

"Some tools that will help at camp, I promise."

"Alright, put it in my bag and take these swords."

Naoko did as he was told and placed the box inside Kenji's satchel. He slung the swords over his shoulder and still had his hands free.

"Time to go."

Kenji left the shop the way they came in and entered the alley once more.

"We left the rope with Jiro. What was your plan for getting back out again?" Naoko sounded concerned.

"There are two of us so we'll boost each other back up to the roof and jump back to the wall."

"Just like that?"

"Yes, why not?"

"You know I don't typically do this sort of thing, right?"

"There's a first time for everything. Come on, if we're quick we can get back up before the guard comes back this way."

Kenji overlapped his hands and put them out as a platform for Naoko. Shaking his head Naoko stepped his foot onto Kenji's hands and Kenji boosted him high enough so he could get a hold of the roof. Naoko pulled himself up but needed Kenji to push on his feet to clamber onto the roof. Naoko knelt down and stuck his hand down for Kenji who jumped up and grabbed a hold of it to hoist himself up and join Naoko.

"Now for the hard part." Kenji said.

"Right." Naoko panted.

After checking for the guard who was currently absent, Kenji took a running start and jumped the gap to grab onto the edge of the wall. After pulling himself up he turned to watch Naoko who had already begun to run. Naoko leapt from the roof and caught onto the wall just as Kenji had done. With a grunt Naoko pulled himself up and rolled onto his back in front of Kenji.

"This is not the time for a nap." Kenji said smiling.

"Let's just go."

The pair scurried across the wall and back to where they had climbed over. Kenji scanned the treeline for any sign of Jiro and right on cue, he came running out from the forest. Jiro's back foot left the grass as he threw the rope up to Kenji who had to lean over the edge to catch it. Kenji tied the rope back up and waved Naoko forward as he watched for the guard who he could now see in the distance returning to their position. He needed to speed this up. Kenji followed closely behind Naoko who was half way down the wall.

"Hey Jiro, catch him."

Kenji unhooked the rope causing both him and Naoko to fall down back to the grass. Kenji rolled as he made contact with the ground and stumbled back to his feet. Jiro and Naoko clumsily got back up after crashing into each other. Naoko looked at Kenji, arms in the air and a slightly annoyed look on his face. Kenji smiled and the trio ran back into the darkness of the forest.

As the men made it back to camp, most of the group was already up and about, settling in to complete tasks and chores. The kids were seated in a circle near the entrance to the cave turning bundles of grass into balls and tossing them at each other. Hanako was on the outskirts gathering berries from some nearby bushes with some of the other women and smiled as she noticed the return of the small group. Jiro and Naoko split off from Kenji, each to their family members who greeted them with relieved smiles and warm embraces. Kenji made his way over to Strider and gave him a pat, for which he received a slobbery greeting. Putting his rope away, Kenji took out the box and journal and placed his satchel back on Strider's saddle. He gave Strider a final rub on his shoulder and walked over to find Saburo and Naoko.

"Ah Kenji, the trip was a success I hear."

"Yes, we came away with more than was planned as well." Kenji said as he placed the box on the ground and handed the journal over to Saburo.

"Oh, my journal, wonderful! With this I can help construct things for the camp. It has all my carpentry notes."

"Excellent. And what about these swords? Did you know they were going to be there?" Kenji took the weapons off his shoulder and placed them in a pile with the ones Naoko had dropped off.

"I wasn't sure, but I didn't want to get your hopes up."

"You have been a tremendous help to this group Saburo. Thank you."

"Don't mention it kid, if it weren't for you, we might not all be here."

"Who should we give swords out to? Who even knows how to handle them?" Naoko questioned.

"That's something we'll have to discuss. I can help train people but I cannot force anyone to carry a weapon who doesn't want to."

"That is a conversation we can have later, and you can count me out of needing a sword." Saburo said. "I'm going to dive into my notes and decide what we could use first."

Saburo left with a wave.

"Naoko, could you do me a favour and put all those swords together inside the cave for now until we decide what to do with them?"

"Sure thing Kenji, and thanks for taking me on that trip."

"No problem, you did well." Kenji gave Naoko a pat on the shoulder and helped him pick up the swords.

"Kenji!" A familiar voice called out.

"Maku! How are things?"

"Good, everyone had a good sleep I think and we had a couple people rotate on watch."

"Excellent, thank you."

"I saw you came back with weapons?" Maku motioned toward Naoko.

"Yes. Found them in Saburo's shop. I figured you and I can help train some of these folks if they want to learn. Better safe than sorry."

"Yes, good to have some extra protection."

"Let's just hope we don't end up needing it."

"Agreed."

"Oh, I almost forgot!" Maku's eyes lit up. "Want some food? I took Kane out and we got some more meat. And some of the women have been gathering berries!"

"That sounds wonderful."

Kenji followed Maku to the campfire that had been set up in the middle of the circle of logs. Chunks of meat had been cooked and left around the fire with berries in a pile next to them.

"Here, a mostly hearty breakfast!" Maku said proud of the meal.

"This is great." Kenji said as he bent down to grab a handful of berries.

"Yes, everyone has done really well at selecting tasks they can do. We all have a job."

"That's great to hear. Later on, we can discuss who the weapons can go out to, and Saburo sounds like he wants to get started on building things for the camp. We'll have lots of work ahead of us."

"That will keep everyone occupied and hopefully keep their minds off things. They will not say much to me, but I can tell everyone's still not one hundred percent after what's happened."

"Can you blame them? We have all been through a lot recently. Perhaps all these tasks will help."

"I hope so."

"So, I don't have to worry about staying up for watch tonight?"

"No, we should be fine, besides you need the rest."

"Yes, I suppose I do."

"Do you want me to gather some of the others who want to learn how to use a sword?"

"Not right now, we'll let everyone enjoy the morning and start later on."

"You're the boss."

"Who told you that?" Kenji gave a look of surprise.

"Well, you are kind of the unelected boss."

"We are all in this group working together. There shouldn't even be a boss."

"Whatever you say boss." Maku gave Kenji a playful punch in the shoulder.

"Shut up."

"So, I'll see you later and we'll train them together?"

"Sure, yes. You know your stuff - you can start without me if I'm not there."

"Alright, we'll see."

The pair parted ways as Kenji's eyes became focused on Saburo who was striding across the grass wielding a small axe. Kenji quickly made his way over to him to investigate.

"Hey Saburo what is that?" Kenji asked gesturing to the axe he was carrying.

"This is an axe my dear boy." Saburo answered holding it up.

"I figured out that much, but what are you planning on doing with it?"

"Nothing, he's doing nothing with it!" Naoko came rushing over.

"Oh yes I am." Saburo retorted.

"Father there are other people here who can do it for you." Naoko pleaded.

"Nonsense, and risk them getting hurt by doing it wrong? No, I'll do it myself."

"What are you going to do?" Kenji interjected.

"My father wants to begin one of his projects, but wants to cut down the tree himself."

"It's my project and I will be the one to do it." Saburo defended.

"How about we help you with the manual labour and you can focus on construction? You'll still have complete control." Kenji suggested.

"I suppose that would be alright. But I'm still cutting down the trees myself." Saburo marched off in search of his first target.

"Sorry, my father always has gotten a little controlling when starting a new project."

"That's alright, I get it. We should help him carry the tree."

"Good idea."

Kenji and Naoko walked over to Saburo who had already hacked several notches into the trunk of a smaller tree. Kenji walked over to one side of Saburo as Naoko did the same, both prepared for whichever way the tree was going to fall. After a handful of swings and more than a few grunts later there was a loud snap from the base of the tree as it toppled to the ground in front of Kenji with an even louder crash, shortly after followed by screams from a couple of the children.

"Saburo you should go make sure the group is prepared for more trees falling. We can carry this back and continue once your back." Kenji said.

"Okay, I'll be right back."

"So, what does your father want to build first?" Kenji asked as he bent down to lift the tree with Naoko.

"He said something about having a roof over the campfire letting us have another spot of shelter outdoors."

"That sounds like a good idea. Count of three: one, two, three."

The pair lifted the tree onto their shoulders and began shuffling back to the center of camp.

"Yes, he seemed to think so. It should help the mood a little at least."

"I agree. Man, this is heavier than I thought." Kenji said between heavy breaths.

"Yes, maybe we should find some of the others."

"Yes, maybe."

With a combined exhale Kenji and Naoko dropped the tree in the middle of camp and began stretching out their arms. Without a cue, some of the other members of the camp came to gather around Saburo who was returning to begin another session of chopping. Kenji smiled as he rubbed his bad shoulder. As the second tree fell, Kenji and Naoko were joined in carrying it back this time making the load feel a lot less troublesome. As Saburo continued to chop, refusing to let anyone else touch his axe, Kenji looked around at the group of people who he had survived with him coming together to complete a task that was too big for any one person.

"Okay, that should be enough for now." Saburo announced, finally lowering his axe.

"Alright, good job everyone! Anyone who wants to learn to use the swords we brought back earlier can go see Maku. He'll start a training session for everyone." Kenji told the working group.

The group began to disperse as Saburo approached Kenji.

"Thanks for the help. I know I can be a bit stubborn when it comes to my trade." Saburo admitted.

"Not a problem, Saburo, I understand. And thanks for getting such a quick start on helping the camp."

"It's the least I can do. I should get to it so hopefully we can have it up by tomorrow."

"Sounds good, just give me a shout if you need anything."

"I will. And thanks again for bringing my things back to me."

"No problem."

Saburo left Kenji to busy himself with his ongoing project while Kenji turned his sights to Maku, who had gathered a group around himself. He had begun handing out swords to members of the group as Kenji approached. Kenji took a spot leaning up against the trunk of a tree as the group began placing themselves in a formation. Maku turned to Kenji with a questioning look in his eye as if to ask if he should begin. Kenji raised his hand motioning toward the participants telling him it was okay to start. Nervously, Maku spun back around to face his students. Kenji watched as Maku went through the stances Ichiro had taught him as a boy years ago. Making sure you had a sturdy stance, a firm grip, and your eyes on your target were all things Ichiro taught, and Maku was reflecting that. As Kenji observed the other group members, he saw them watching Maku as he demonstrated different strikes and then tried to copy him. They were rough around the edges but Kenji knew that for some this was their first time even holding a sword. Most of them were just trying to get used to the weight in their hands. Kenji turned and noticed some of the children coming to watch beside him. He knelt down beside the boy who was sent to retrieve the maggots for Hanako.

"What's your name pal?" Kenji asked the child.

"I'm Jun. That's my father in the front." The boy said pointing to Kane, who was standing within the group.

"Could you do me a favour Jun? I need you to go and find some strong branches for me, about this long." Kenji stuck his arms for measurement.

"Okay!" Jun rushed off seemingly happy to be getting some responsibility.

Kenji stood back up as Maku walked over to him.

"I just have them practicing striking drills. Where'd you send the kid?"

"I sent him to try and find some branches. I thought if they are strong enough we could have them practice on each other."

"Good idea. Am I doing alright so far?"

"Yes, you're doing fine. Don't worry if they don't all get it at first. You know as well as I do that it takes practice."

"I know. I'm going to go over some blocks, let me know when the kid comes back."

"I will."

Maku returned to his students who were awaiting their next instructions. As Kenji watched Maku go over basic blocking techniques he felt a tug on his leg. Jun had returned and was carrying an armful of branches. Happily, the boy dropped the pile of branches next to Kenji and plopped himself down on the grass beside him.

"Thanks Jun, good job." Kenji praised the boy.

Jun was now too fixated on watching his father practice to hear the compliment. Kenji began stripping the branches as best he could, to try to create long smooth pieces of wood to practice with. He was more or less successful and picked one up to test. Swinging it around in his hand, it was not the weight of a normal sword but it would have to do. He just hoped they would hold together when making contact with each other. Putting the makeshift training sword back down Kenji signalled to Maku letting him know they were ready.

"Okay everyone, we are going to put what we've done so far into real application. Kenji has gathered some 'swords' to practice on each other with, so partner up."

The students did as they were told and found a dueling partner.

"Alright, make sure you and your partner have enough space so you will not run into anyone. Once you're ready, practice the overhead strike paired with the block we practiced."

"They seem to be holding together alright." Kenji said as he walked over to the front of the group with Maku.

"Yes, they are. It'll be good for them to practice in partners when we're not around."

"Yes, want me to watch some of the pairs so you can keep an eye on the rest?"

"That would be great, thanks."

Kenji and Maku split off to watch the partners practice with one another. Kenji observed Kane and Jiro together going through the strikes as Maku told them to. As Kenji watched, Jiro blocked Kane's strike but lost his footing under the pressure landing on the ground. Kane was helping Jiro up as Kenji arrived.

"The block was placed right but you need a stronger stance. Allow your knees to be bent as the strike hits so they can absorb some of the impact. Just be careful not to bend too low. May I?" Kenji reached out for Jiro's practice sword.

Kenji took the sword from Jiro and turned to face Kane, readying his stance.

"Alright, try that strike again, but Jiro, watch my legs."

Kane wound the sword up above his head and brought it down onto Kenji's block. At the point of impact Kenji braced himself and he allowed his legs to absorb the strike.

"Good strong strike, now you try." Kenji said passing the weapon back to Jiro.

Kenji stood back as Kane repeated his strike this time to Jiro. This time Jiro brought his sword up to block but bent his knees a little as the strike hit, allowing him to hold his ground.

"That's it, well done. Keep practicing." Kenji applauded Jiro.

The duo thanked Kenji and continued on with their practice as he left to watch the other students.

"How's everything coming along?" Hanako approached Kenji with curiosity.

"I think they are doing fine for their first time. Maku's doing well teaching them." Kenji replied.

"Why aren't you teaching them?" Hanako questioned.

"Maku is perfectly capable, I enjoy helping where he needs it."

"Why are you so against taking leadership of this group?"

"There's that leadership talk again, Maku brought it up already. We all work together and I'm no leader." Kenji said defensively.

"That's not how the others see it. They are fine working together but they need leadership from you. Even if you don't think you can deliver it."

"They would do fine if I wasn't here."

"I don't think you even believe yourself. Sure, we could have survived a couple of days but what happens if soldiers attack? How would we defend ourselves?"

"I cannot lead these people; you're better suited for it. And besides, they all know you and your mother."

"They know you now; you've done a lot of good for these people. You brought them together." Hanako argued.

"They were together already and would be if I hadn't done anything."

"You know what I mean." Hanako sighed. "So, are you actually going to get some rest tonight?" Hanako asked trying to change the subject.

"We'll see. I'd feel better if I stayed up to watch."

"You don't have to be the hero all the time. Why else are you training the others?"

"Self defense."

"Well I would advise you get some rest. You're going to need it if you are the boss around here."

"You sound like Maku." Kenji laughed.

"I thought you might get tired of listening to me." Hanako teased.

"Not yet. But don't push it."

"Fine, I'll spare you and go check on dinner."

"Sounds good."

Kenji watched Hanako walk away and then looked up past the trees and into the sky. The sun had begun to creep downwards without Kenji's notice. *Did I not eat lunch?* Kenji began to rub his stomach. *Too many things to do.* Kenji walked over to the campfire where Saburo was busy putting some of the cut down trees into the ground, to act as posts. The small wooden box Kenji had brought back with Naoko was opened beside Saburo and he was chipping away at the bottom of the trees trying to wedge them into the dirt. Kenji took a spot on one of the logs and ate some leftover venison as Saburo tirelessly worked on his task.

"You're sure you don't need help with anything Saburo?" Kenji asked swallowing the last of his food.

"No, it's alright. Once these posts are in, I'm going to take a break. My back doesn't seem as able to handle long periods of work as well as it used to."

"Well you know where to find me." Kenji left to go search the cave for a spot to sleep later on.

He ducked to enter the cave and took his first actual step inside since they had arrived. The cave was surprisingly open and even more so once he was inside. Kenji found a spot against the rock wall near one of the back corners. He sat down to lean against it and decide whether it's where he would sleep that night. He let his head rest back against the smooth wall and his eyes began to get heavy. He shook his head trying to loosen his eyelids but that seemed to cause them to rebel and close even more. Next thing he knew Kenji let out a yawn and made himself comfortable against the wall of the cave.

CHAPTER 14

~Five Days Later~

Kenji woke up to the sounds of a busy camp. Before he even lifted his head from where he slept, he could hear the children splashing in the pond, giving the parents an early morning cleaning job. He heard the sounds of people talking and rushing around the clearing, busying themselves with daily tasks and chores. Kenji sat up and stretched his arms giving some extra attention to the shoulder injury he could barely feel anymore. He picked his swords up from beside him and after inspecting each one, placed them on his back. As he left the cover of the cave, he threw up his hand to shield his eyes from the morning sun. He walked over to the campfire which was surrounded by the food the group had gathered and was now sheltered by a wooden roof constructed by Saburo just days before. Picking up a handful of assorted berries and stuffing them in his mouth he sat down next to Saburo who was seemingly admiring his work.

"You did well with this structure Saburo. It held up well in the rain last night." Kenji complimented.

"Thank you, Kenji, I told you it would." Saburo replied while rubbing one of the posts.

"I never doubted you for a second."

"I've been trying to decide what to build next for us, perhaps a hitching post for your horse there." Saburo said motioning toward Strider who was freely trotting around the edge of camp.

"That would be nice."

"It would not take me too long but I heard a rumour you weren't planning on keeping it around."

"That's a harder decision to make than I would have thought." Kenji admitted.

"So, you want me to start on the hitching post?" Saburo asked looking for some more work.

"Yes, you can, it'll help. Thanks, Saburo."

"My pleasure."

"I'm going to make the rounds and check on the others. Take care."

"You as well Kenji."

Kenji waved his goodbye and walked out toward the edge of camp and began his now standard patrol along the perimeter. Greeting members of the group as he walked along, Kenji made a full loop around the outside of the camp observing the hardworking members keeping themselves busy. As he finished his tour of camp Kenji was approached by Haru, Kane's wife, and she was followed closely by Jun.

"Hello, how are you this morning?" Kenji smiled as they approached.

"We're well. I was actually wondering if I could ask you a favour."

"Of course, what do you need?"

"The kids were playing in the pond this morning and got pretty muddy. They are all cleaned up now but I was hoping you would be willing to take them out to play a cleaner game."

"I think I heard some of that this morning when I got up. I'll take them out behind the cave."

"Oh, thank you Kenji!"

"My pleasure. I'll see if I can drain some of this energy out of them."

"If you do, you'll have to teach me that trick." Haru laughed.

"Ha, I will. Jun, could you help me and get the other kids to join us behind the cave?"

"I'll be super fast Kenji, just you watch!" Jun sped off in search of the other children.

"I best get going and find something to help with. Thanks again Kenji."

"No problem."

The two parted with a wave and Kenji jogged off behind the cave to find the kids had already managed to beat him there.

"See Kenji, I told you I'd be fast!" Jun boasted.

"And you were right. So, who wants to play some hide and seek?"

"Yes!" came a unanimous answer.

"Alright, but I have to warn you, back in my village I was the undefeated champion."

"You'll never be able to find us!" challenged Aiko.

"We'll see about that! I'll count to twenty and you all go and find a place to hide!"

Kenji turned his back on the children and put his face to the cave wall. Staring into the rock face Kenji could hear the children's scurrying feet as they scrambled to find hiding spots. Kenji began to count as he thought about the countless times he used to make Ichiro play this game with him, even when he did not really want to.

"...nineteen, and twenty! Ready or not, here I come!"

Kenji turned back to face the forest that was now teeming with hiding children. Kenji set out to find his first child. Looking down at his feet there were numerous different paths created by the children, he just had to decide which one he wanted to follow. Kenji decided on a trail of footprints to his right and set off to follow it. As he walked along the trail left by the unknown child, Kenji scanned the area around him making sure he did not miss any extra children off to his sides. He came up on a part of the trail that hooked hard to the left and stopped behind the wide trunk of a tree. Kenji knelt crouched down and slowly made his way around the side.

"Found you!" Kenji announced by throwing his arms out in front of him.

"Oh, you did! Can I help find the others?" Asked Aiko.

"Sure you can, want to lead the way?"

"Yes!" Aiko set off with determination looking for the remaining players.

"Wait for me!" Kenji had to break into a jog to catch up to the enthusiastic Aiko.

Suddenly Aiko stopped and went low to the grass. She turned toward Kenji and put one finger up to her lips signalling for Kenji to stay quiet. Kenji crouched and made his way up to Aiko. Aiko put her hands out toward Kenji telling him he was not as quiet as she wanted.

"I think I see Kin behind that bush." Aiko whispered while pointing toward a bush a couple of metres away from them.

Aiko had good eyesight. Kenji could see Kin kneeling down behind the same bush she was pointing at. Kin was the brother of Etsu, both of whom Kenji had met on the third day the camp had stayed in the clearing. They had young parents, Fuyu and Isas, who had met when Isas was a farmhand just outside of Sekigahara. They had already had their children when Isas and his family were forced inside the walls upon the arrival of Tokugawa and his army.

"Want to go get him?" Kenji asked.

"Yes, but remember to stay quiet." Aiko emphasized.

"I will."

Kenji followed Aiko as the two of them snuck up on Kin and surprised him on the other side of the bush.

"Aw man! I thought I was so hidden."

"Want to join us? We're going to find Jun and your sister now," said Aiko, who had happily taken charge.

"Yes, let's do it!"

The trio set off in search of the two remaining players. Kin found his sister fairly quickly after hearing her laughter come from behind a fallen log. After Etsu joined, Aiko regained control of her search party and they went off in search of Jun who was now the final player left to find. After moving a short distance back in the direction of camp Kenji felt a tap on his shoulder. He turned to see Jun who had revealed himself.

"Oh Jun, we were just looking for you. Why did you come out?"

"There are people in the forest."

Kenji's eyes immediately started scanning around his group as he listened to Jun.

"I was hiding real good when I thought I heard you all coming so I peeked out to check but instead it wasn't you."

"Who was it, Jun?" Kenji stayed crouched but kept his eyes surveying the trees.

"They looked like the men who were chasing us before we went to the cave. I got scared and ran to find you."

"That's good Jun. You did the right thing. What direction were they in?"

Jun lifted a finger to point past Kenji's shoulder and back toward the camp.

"Okay children, the game's over. Now I need you all to listen very carefully. We need to head back to camp together. You need to stay very close to me and do what I say, alright?"

"But what if the bad men find us?" Etsu questioned, her voice slightly trembling.

"Just stay close to me and we'll all be alright."

Kenji stood up now and made sure all the children were grouped behind him. The group began to make their way back to camp as Kenji tried to watch every tree looking for soldiers that might see them. Suddenly, as he heard the rustle of leaves beside him, a soldier jumped out and grabbed Kenji trapping both his arms by his sides. As Kenji struggled to loosen the hold Aiko gave the man a swift kick in the shin causing him to loosen just enough for Kenji to turn out and throw an elbow into his jaw. The man stumbled back before resetting to take another swing at Kenji. As he swung with his right arm, Kenji timed his duck and came up behind him, using his own arm to wrap his opponent's arm up alongside his neck. Kenji gave the man a strong kick to the back of his leg causing him to fall to his knees and allowing Kenji to grab his other arm and wrap it behind the soldier's head, tightening up the choke. The man struggled in Kenji's grip, trying to swing his other arm in an attempt to unsheathe his sword. Kenji responded by hooking his legs around the man's abdomen trapping his other arm to his body.

"Children, turn away, but stay right there."

The children did as Kenji instructed and looked away as the soldier continued to struggle against Kenji's choke. Kenji tightened his grip and tucked his head down atop the man's shoulder as he could feel his opponent getting weaker. Soon the soldier's body went limp and Kenji released him causing him to fall to the grass next to him. Kenji was breathing heavy as he stood again and faced the kids.

"Okay, run toward the cave, but stop when we get there okay? I'll be right beside you."

Again the children obeyed and took off running back toward the cave with Kenji jogging up alongside them. As they neared the back of the cave Kenji could hear yelling with the clang of metal coming from the camp and unsheathed both his swords. The group stopped at the backside of the cave as Kenji told them to.

"Okay, now I need to go help the others and when I run out there, I need all of you to run inside the cave and stay there until one of us comes to get you, alright?"

The children nodded together.

"Ready? Go!"

The children followed Kenji around the side of the cave and dove one by one inside the entrance. Turning quick to ensure they made it inside Kenji turned back to see a soldier running right at him, sword raised. Kenji parried the strike with his left sword and swung with his right toward the man's neck causing him to fall to the dirt as a spray of blood covered Kenji's face. Unshaken, Kenji continued into the camp toward Jiro who was holding one of the swords and was engaged with another soldier as his wife Riku was behind him. Kenji rushed to aid Jiro but as he got there Jiro blocked an overhead strike and as he pushed back countered by thrusting his sword through the man's stomach. Another soldier was approaching though and Jiro was struggling to pull his sword out of his toppled opponent. Kenji ran forward, driving his shoulder into the attacker, and with a small recoil thrust his swords up and out the top of the man's back. Pulling hard to regain both of his swords, Kenji turned around to face Riku and Jiro who had successfully gotten his sword back.

"You're alright?"

"Yes, I've got her!" Jiro said in between heavy breaths.

Kenji ran toward the campfire now where Fuyu and Isas were being approached by two more soldiers. Kenji push kicked the first soldier, giving him room to step in between him and the couple. Kenji threw the first strike and slashed his sword up under the soldier's armpit, finishing by thrusting his other sword into the center of the man's chest. He turned his head as the first man ran back at him, but before he could make contact Maku rushed in and dispatched him placing his back against Kenji's.

"Four more coming at us!" Kenji called.

"I see them!"

Maku was the first to have contact as his soldier tried to slash across his chest but he responded by parrying and jabbing his sword back into the soldier. Kenji's first opponent rushed him and locked swords against him. Kenji braced to take the block and felt Maku pushing against him to give him added support. Maku engaged with his second opponent as Kenji kicked the man swiftly in the groin causing him to curl over, leaving an opening for Kenji to jam his sword down into the man's back. Pulling the sword out, Kenji readied himself as his final opponent charged toward him. Maku blocked his soldiers' incoming attack and drove his man's sword into the ground allowing him to give him an elbow followed up by a slash across his back to dispatch him.

"Kenji, duck!"

Kenji responded and turned his shoulder down toward his running attacker as Maku spun around using Kenji's back as a level and drove his sword right between the soldiers' eyes with one arm. The fourth opponent fell to the grass as a scream was let out by Hanako, who was trapped up against a tree by the final soldier in camp. Kenji took off in a sprint but knew he would not be able to get there in time.

"Kenji, catch!"

Kenji's head swivelled to see Saburo who had thrown him his hand axe. He dropped his sword and caught the axe not stopping to lose stride. Kenji cocked his arm back and hurled the axe through the air watching as it split the back of the soldiers' skull, causing him to fall forward onto Hanako. With another scream she pushed the man's corpse off of her and to the ground.

Kenji slowed to a stop and dropped his other sword, putting his hands on his hips. He was quick enough to save Hanako's life but soon realized that not everyone had shared the same fate. As Kenji approached Hanako he could see another body down next to her. Cho's body was lying lifeless in the grass, blood seeping from a stab wound in her stomach. Hanako knelt down beside Cho as Kenji walked over and put a hand on her shoulder. Before Kenji could try and comfort Hanako a scream came from the opposite side of camp. Kenji rushed over to find Jun's mother Haru sitting down beside another body in the dirt. Kane was leaning up against the trunk of a tree. There was a long diagonal slash across his chest. The scream he had heard came from Haru.

"Kenji, you have to help me! Help my husband!" Haru desperately pleaded.

But Kane's wound was too deep and too large, Kenji knew this. He stood over Kane as he looked up at Kenji, his eyes still clinging to the small amount of life he had left.

"Kenji, I don't feel too good." Kane said his voice raspy and slow. "I don't think I'm going to make it."

"No Kane, don't say that! You have me and Jun! You'll be okay!" Haru began sobbing into Kane's shoulder.

"Kenji, tell me the truth." Kane looked up to Kenji again.

All Kenji could manage was to shake his head confirming to Kane what he thought to be true.

"No, how can you say that! If you were here earlier you could have saved him!" Haru screamed putting Kenji to blame.

Kenji had no response but to look to the ground, desperately wishing there was still something he could do.

"Don't put this on him… There was no more he…" Kane took a deep breath in. "I love you, look after Jun."

Kane began to cough, blood spraying with each exhale. As he reached up to put his hand against Haru's collarbone he shut his eyes and his body went limp. Kenji stumbled backwards as Haru burst into tears over top of her husband's body. Kenji felt a stabling hand on his shoulder and turned his eyes to see Saburo.

"We should bury them, properly."

Kenji nodded in agreement.

"You have to know you did all you could."

Kenji turned away from Saburo and walked back to where he had left his swords. Leaning over to pick them up Kenji's eyes became locked to them. He stared at his weapons now covered with the blood of the soldiers that lay around him. He looked around at the camp now littered with bodies. The sounds of chores being done and children playing had been replaced by crying and pain.

"Mother? Mother, what happened to mother?"

Kenji spun around terrified from the voice he heard. Aiko came walking toward him, her eyes focused past him toward her mother who was lying cold beside Hanako.

"Mother, can you hear me?"

As Aiko drew closer her eyes changed as the reality struck her. She toppled down on top of her mother, soaking her shirt as she cried. Hanako took Aiko and hugged her tight as she continued to cry. Maku and Jiro solemnly made their way to them and picked up Cho's body. Kenji collapsed to the grass and put his head between his knees.

CHAPTER 15

As the last of the soldiers' bodies had been dragged away, the distraught group gathered together on the edge of the pond. Kenji stood off to the side of the pond looking down toward the two stone piles that had been placed to cover the fallen group members. More tears were shared between them as Saburo stepped forward to address everyone.

"Kane and Cho were dearly loved. We may not have all had deep connections to the lost but that changed as we became a family within this forest. And so we mourn together as one family. We live on now to honour those who we have lost today and vow to never forget them in our future."

After bowing his head, Saburo stepped back to his place in the crowd. The silent group stood gathered for a while longer before slowly dispersing around the camp once more. Kenji walked out to the edge of the clearing and pulled out one of his swords. Taking his rag out he began to slowly rub the length of the blade trying to clear away the blood. As he continued to clean his weapon he stared out toward a point beyond the forest as if trying to see the walls of Sekigahara once again. As he looked past the walls and into the courtyard Kenji saw himself standing alone in the center watching as Tokugawa walked out to meet him. He clenched his fist as Tokugawa drew closer then quickly released before squeezing too tight around his blade. He switched to his second blade as Maku came up behind him.

He continued to look out toward the forest as Maku took a spot next to him.

"The group has gathered by the campfire, they want to talk about what comes next. They want you there."

"Tell them I'll be there in a moment. Are the children with them?"

"Yes, Jun is with his mother but Aiko refuses to come. She will not leave the cave or talk to anyone."

"Let them know I'll be there soon."

"Okay, are you alright?"

"I'm fine. I'll be there soon."

"Okay." Maku retreated to go and relay the message.

Kenji sheathed his second blade upon his back and stuffed the rag away. He turned around, not in the direction of the fire but toward the cave. As Kenji approached the entrance he ducked down to look inside. The inside was darker toward the back but Kenji could make out where Aiko had positioned herself, lying down under a small overhang against the back wall. Kenji entered slowly and walked quietly toward the child.

"Go away!" Aiko said hearing Kenji approach.

"Aiko I just want to talk." Kenji held his hands out in front of him.

"Well I don't want to!" Aiko retorted.

"Aiko, I know what's happened is hard, I don't want you to be alone in here."

"I don't want to see anyone." Aiko sobbed.

"Aiko, I know what you're going through. I can help. It helps to talk to someone."

"How can you know what it's like?"

Kenji took a seat beside Aiko.

"I lost both of my parents when I was young too. All I had was my uncle after. But now he's gone too."

Aiko sat up slightly, wiping some tears from her cheeks.

"What happened to your uncle?"

"A bad man killed him not long before I met you all."

"Why didn't you tell us? I thought you said it helps to talk to people." Aiko questioned.

"You're one of the only people who know. I chose to keep it to myself because I thought it would be better that way. But it doesn't help to keep it locked inside. After I met all of you, I wanted to run away on my own, but it felt good to be part of a group."

"Are you still sad about your mother and father? And your uncle?"

"All the time, but it is nice to have people around you who can be with you, just like you have."

Aiko sat up and wrapped her arms around Kenji in a tight squeeze and began crying again into his chest.

"I miss her so much Kenji. I want her back."

"I know Aiko, I know." Kenji put his arms around her and began to rub her back.

"There are people here who care for you, just like Saburo said. We are a family now."

"What… are we going to do?" Aiko said in between heavy breaths.

"That's what we were going to talk about outside. But I didn't want you left out. Do you want to come help us decide?" Kenji wiped a tear that had rolled down Aiko's face.

"Okay, can I sit with you?"

"Of course you can."

Aiko sat back up and took a deep breath. She held out her hand for Kenji. Kenji stood and took her hand as they walked out of the cave together. As the two of them made their way over to the campfire it was surrounded by mixed emotions and an argument that had already started. Kenji took a seat in between Maku and Hanako and sat with his knees together so Aiko could hop on. Kenji could feel the anger and sadness around him and knew the argument was going to escalate.

"How can you suggest we stay here? Did you not see what just happened! Two of our own were slaughtered!" Jiro was standing up yelling across the fire.

"But where are we going to go? Surely the soldiers will keep looking for us," Naoko, who was sitting in between his mother and father, shot back.

"I agree we cannot stay here. But we need a plan of what to do. I need to make sure Fuyu and my kids are safe." Isas responded.

"That's what we are here to talk about, but we all need to stay calm and talk about this rationally." Hanako interjected.

"We need a plan now!" Jiro argued.

"Does anyone have any suggestions?" Maku asked the group.

"We could try and find another village away from the city. Live peacefully there, away from the fighting." Nami suggested.

"Surely a group of our size will raise attention walking into a village." Haru said while Jun was curled up in her lap.

"What about starting our own village? We could find a nice spot and start to build up?" Nami suggested.

"Does anyone here really want to live under Tokugawa?" Maku brought up.

The group pondered this for a moment.

"What do you suggest we do then?" Jiro asked.

"We could leave Japan; find someplace new for us to settle."

"Are you kidding?" Jiro shouted.

"Maku, we cannot leave our home!" Saburo protested.

"And how are we supposed to get our kids out of here?" Fuyu asked.

"Think about it. What's left for any of you here? I know for me it's only bad memories and I don't want to be living under the rule of the man who took everything from us."

"What have you lost, traitor?" Jiro pointed a finger over the flames now. "You attacked our city and now you think you are one of us?"

Kenji's eyes narrowed as he watched the situation get more out of control.

"I was taken from my village! I didn't have a choice but to fight under him!" Maku stood up and shouted back.

"If you fought so much then why didn't you train us better? If you did then maybe Kane would still be alive and she would still have a mother!" Jiro pointed down to Aiko who began to cry into Kenji's chest.

"Jiro, that's enough!" Hanako interrupted. "This is not what we need to be arguing about right now. We need a plan to go forward."

Kenji put a hand out onto Maku's leg telling him it was time to sit down. Jiro continued to stand.

"If we do leave Japan how do we get away? This is an island." Riku asked, giving her input for the first time.

"We would need a ship large enough to fit all of us." Isas said.

Aiko had stopped crying and sat back up in Kenji's lap looking at him. Kenji was too focused on the talk to notice her. So she began tugging on his shirt to get his attention. As the group members continued to try and come up with a plan Aiko whispered her suggestion into Kenji's ear. He smiled and rubbed Aiko's arm.

"Nagoya." Kenji announced.

"That's fairly far south Kenji. And how would we get a ship out of there?" Saburo questioned.

"Aiko says her father used to know a man in the port and would often rent a ship to go fishing. She says it was practically his."

"That could work. Where would we go after that?" Hanako asked.

"I'm not sure, perhaps a smaller island off the coast?"

"That will not be under Tokugawa's jurisdiction?" Naoko asked.

"Perhaps farther then, any ideas?" Kenji addressed the group.

"I don't think we should be going anywhere with him." Jiro butted in motioning back to Maku.

"Hey, I've been out here surviving with you all this time. I'm on your side." Maku objected.

"For all we know he could have led them here! He could be a spy!"

Maku stood up to defy Jiro.

"That's absurd; you are just emotional from today."

"Why aren't you? Is it because you are working for them?" Jiro stood up in protest.

Maku stormed past the fire to stand in Jiro's face. Kenji patted Aiko on the shoulder and she got up allowing him to stand up as well.

"I don't have to take this from you!"

"Get away from me!" Jiro yelled shoving Maku to the ground.

Maku hit the dirt next to the fire causing his sleeve to catch flame. He rolled over frantically to put it out and Kenji moved around the fire in front of Jiro.

"What do you want now?"

"That's enough Jiro, sit down and let's talk this through." Kenji said, staring back into his eyes.

"Why do you defend him? For all you know he could be the reason your uncle is dead!"

Kenji's fist clenched and his eyes narrowed. The rest of the camp went silent and Maku sat up having put out the flame.

"Yes, I heard your uncle got killed; maybe he told them to do it?" Jiro taunted.

"Sit down Jiro." Kenji spoke through clenched teeth.

"Make me."

"You don't want that."

"I thought you were a good fighter?"

"Jiro, stop. That's enough." Riku pleaded to her husband.

"You should listen to her."

"Who made you leader anyway? Shouldn't you earn it?"

"I'm just like you - I'm no one's leader. Now stand down."

"I don't take orders from you!"

Jiro threw a jab straight out toward Kenji's nose. Kenji slipped his head out of the way and parried his arm aside. This only angered Jiro more, who retaliated by throwing another punch, this time an uppercut toward Kenji's chin. Kenji stepped back out of the way and pushed an opened hand square into Jiro's chest causing him to stumble backward. Jiro's rage grew and he unsheathed his sword from his belt. Kenji bent his knees and readied himself.

"You don't want to do this."

Some of the group members covered their faces. Jiro raised his sword up and struck downward aiming for the top of Kenji's head. Kenji side stepped the attack blocking his wrist hard with his left arm and causing Jiro to lose his grip on the sword. As the sword fell, Kenji moved forward and stuck out his right arm wrapping his fingers around Jiro's neck. Jiro gasped and tried to grab at Kenji's hand as Kenji stared back at his beaten foe. Kenji stared into Jiro's eyes but what he saw was not respect. It was fear. Kenji's eyes widened and he let go of Jiro's neck causing him to collapse to the grass, struggling to gain back his breath. He turned to the other members of the group who were silently staring back at him, their eyes wide. Aiko was hiding behind the log beside Hanako her small eyes looking back at Kenji. Kenji looked back at Jiro who had Riku kneeling over him on the ground. He unclenched his fist and left toward the cave.

Kenji stormed through the entrance to the cave and sat back against the wall. Laying his arms on his knees he rested his head against the stone and closed his eyes. He took a deep breath and reviewed in his mind what had just happened. *Did you take it too far? Was that the right response? Maybe it was, but what will the others think of you now?* Kenji pounded his fist back against the cave wall and shook off the pain. Not a word came from the campfire and he wondered if they were all still sitting around it together. Kenji shook his head and looked at his feet, thinking they probably did not want him on this trip anymore. Maybe they did not want him in the first place. Before he could decide on an answer a figure filled the entrance to the cave.

"He was just emotional from the day we had, I cannot blame him. He'll cool off by morning."

Hanako came and sat next to Kenji turning her head to look at him.

"Did I take it too far?"

"What do you think?" Hanako countered.

"I don't know. Maybe I shouldn't have choked him. I wasn't going to kill him."

"I know but he drew a sword on you. The way I see it he's lucky to be alive. You showed mercy."

"I shouldn't have let it escalate."

"That was out of your hands. Like I said he was emotional, before you and Aiko arrived, he was already stirring up trouble."

"I'm not coming with you to Nagoya in the morning."

"What? Why not?" Hanako asked in shock.

"I'm going to go back to the city to buy all of you some time. Make sure you get a head start from the soldiers."

"You cannot, the group needs you on the journey."

"Where are you going?" Another voice filled the cave.

The pair looked up to see Aiko walking toward them.

"Why can't you come with us?"

"Aiko, I need to go back to the city. I'll come back once I'm done there."

"He wants to give us a good shot of getting ahead of the soldiers." Hanako said.

"But I want you to come with us." Aiko said.

"I will come back and meet you before you get there, I promise."

"What if you're not?"

"He will be. Don't worry." Hanako tried to reassure Aiko.

"Hanako, could I have a second to talk to Kenji?"

Kenji and Hanako looked at each other in slight surprise.

"Sure, I'll start helping the others pack up before bed." Hanako smiled and left the cave.

Aiko sat down in front of Kenji and crossed her legs putting her hands in her lap.

"What is it Aiko?" Kenji asked intrigued.

"Why are you really going to the city?" Aiko questioned.

"You heard. I'm going to buy you some time to get far away from the soldiers."

"I don't believe you."

Kenji chuckled.

"Oh yes, and why is that?"

"I think you are going there for a different reason but that reason will still help us get farther away."

"How old are you?" Kenji asked smiling.

"I'm ten." Aiko said confidently.

"Well Aiko I wasn't lying, I'm going to buy you some time but I have a plan on how to do it."

"But you also have another reason to go. So, you were only partly telling the truth."

"I guess you're right. But I'll be back to join you all on the way there, like I said."

"Kenji?"

"Yes?"

"Are you going to kill the man who attacked our city?"

Kenji was taken back by the bluntness of her question.

"Well…yes I am."

"Oh, okay." Aiko looked at the ground before looking back to Kenji. "And you're going to win?"

"As I said, I will be back to join you tomorrow."

"I believe you."

"I'm glad. You should help pack up and then get some rest. You have a big day tomorrow."

Kenji stood up and Aiko did the same. As Aiko left toward the exit she stopped and turned again.

"I hope you win Kenji."

Aiko turned and exited the cave, leaving Kenji alone once more. After staring at the entrance awhile Kenji left as well to go and find Strider. As he approached, Strider neighed in happiness and Kenji gave him a pat on the neck. Kenji made sure his few supplies were inside the satchel and tightened his swords to his back. After turning to look at the others, who were too busy packing up to notice him, he took a deep breath and departed into the forest.

CHAPTER 16

Kenji listened to the sounds of the forest as he walked, sounds of creatures scurrying to find a place to sleep, or the chirping of birds as they called goodnight across the treetops. He looked down at his feet that were stepping quickly but quietly as if he was trying not to disturb the ground. He had already walked this path many times before. He rubbed his shoulder, remembering the hunting trip he and Maku went on. He could still hear the sound of the arrow being released and flying through the air before piercing the deer they found. He heard the thump the deer made as it collapsed to the grass and remembered the pain in his injured shoulder that Maku noticed even though he tried to act tough. He had walked this path with Jiro and Kane and recalled having to listen to Jiro's life story and Kane failing to catch Jiro as they jumped from the wall after grabbing Saburo's tools. The last thing he had said to Jiro was a threat and the last words spoken between he and Kane would be Kane's last. Kenji pictured the city he would soon see, the city that for some reason he found himself always coming back to. The city that had taken everything from him. He envisioned walking down the main street and up toward the palace doors, walking to the courtyard and meeting his foe in the centre. Kenji knew exactly what his uncle would say but pushed the thought out of his head as he was getting closer to the edge of the forest. He could see the walls through the trees now and rested his arm out on the trunk of a tree as he approached the edge of the woods.

He looked up to the top of the wall and could see himself repelling down after his first time inside the city, the first time he met Hanako after his failed mission to kill Mitsunari. Kenji stayed just inside the treeline as he walked the edge of the forest toward the front of the city. As he made it to the front of the city, he stared out at the field now shrouded in pain and anguish. So many lives were lost on this ground and Kenji wondered how long the memory of it would last before it was turned back into farming fields. Kenji stepped out of the forest and walked up to the front of the city, stopping in front of the gates and folding his hands down in front of him. The gates almost seemed bigger now that they had been repaired and Kenji could not help but admire the speed at which they had been put back together as they towered over him. As Kenji waited patiently, he could see men rushing toward the wall, pulling arrows back in their bows as he stared directly at the gates. But before any arrows were loosed another soldier approached the wall and signalled for the archers to stand down and for the gates to be opened. Just as Kenji had hoped he had been recognized. As the gates began to open, Kenji stared past them and down the street to his destination. He let his hands drop back to his sides and entered the city. While he walked past the gates, he could see soldiers lining up on either side of him, not attacking but still having their hands over the hilts of their swords. Making his way further down the street, citizens began joining the soldiers out beside him as he got closer to the courtyard. Kenji made the same walk he had made when the city was in flames and he was walking beside a man who he now called his enemy. As Kenji reached the courtyard there was a darkness that engulfed it. He turned his head to look up at the clouds that had connected to form an ominous blockade in front of the moon. As he neared the center of the square, the door of the palace slid open revealing the reason he had come. Tokugawa's shoulders nearly filled the entire doorway. His freshly cleaned armour was glistening, the emblem that bore his sigil proudly covering his breastplate. As he stepped down the stairs joining Kenji in the courtyard, Kenji could see movement in his peripherals. Bodies had begun to appear around the courtyard, an eager audience, but Kenji was not sure for whom they were cheering. A mixture of Tokugawa's soldiers and the civilians who remained in the city were lining the square surrounding the event in the center. The stone square had an ornate design in the middle, and Tokugawa stood on its' edge. Kenji stepped up to the opposite side of the design to stand parallel to him. Kenji looked Tokugawa in the eyes, the eyes of the man who took his uncle away from him. He stepped his feet together and without breaking eye contact with Tokugawa, Kenji bent slowly at the waist. When his back was straight again Kenji took a deep breath in and let his shoulders relax for a moment. Tokugawa looked back on Kenji and a quiet chatter had begun to form in the crowd around them. Tokugawa straightened his shoulders and stepped his feet together. The crowd was silent as Tokugawa returned the bow to Kenji and straightened again to face him. Kenji knew Tokugawa was too honourable to not have returned his sign of respect but there was still a part of him that was surprised. Kenji closed his eyes and took another deep breath in as he reached back with his right arm and grasped the handle of his sword. Tokugawa did the same and the pair unsheathed their swords leaving them hanging by their sides. Kenji stepped back with his right foot and took his sword in both hands, now letting his right hand rest on top of his left. He raised his sword up to his head perfectly splitting Tokugawa in his vision in front of him. As Kenji lowered his sword slightly to point above Tokugawa's head he turned his feet to point past Tokugawa's left shoulder. Tokugawa looked back at Kenji now matching his opponent's stance and with his right foot stepped back so his feet were pointing past Kenji's left shoulder. In unison the pair took one step closer to one another, not once breaking eye contact. Kenji could smell Tokugawa's breath on the air now and he was sure Tokugawa could smell his. Kenji watched as Tokugawa's eyes narrowed slightly as he tightened his grip.

Raising his sword back above his head, Tokugawa stepped toward Kenji, slashing straight down on top of him. Kenji reacted by raising his sword up to be parallel with the ground and lowering his stance as his shoulders felt the impact of his opponents first strike. The connection of metal rang throughout the city as Kenji pushed back against Tokugawa's opening strike and stepped off to his right, repositioning his sword in front of his face. Tokugawa had already recovered and had turned to face Kenji. Kenji glided forward, next releasing his grip with his left hand and jabbing out with his right. Tokugawa leaned out to his left and brought his sword down to parry away the strike, leaning just enough so he could step out afterwards to recover. Kenji's arm was forced off to his left leaving his shoulder vulnerable, causing him to step his left foot in a spin over his left shoulder so he could face Tokugawa again. Tokugawa raised his arms up once again, this time striking down toward Kenji's right shoulder. Kenji brought his sword over to block the initial strike, but Tokugawa followed it with a second and third strike, each time alternating shoulders. Kenji stepped his left foot back to shift his sword over and stepped back once more so he could do the same on his right. After the last connection on his right side, Kenji pushed Tokugawa's sword past his right arm and leaned back only to shift his weight forward again, allowing for a follow up slash across Tokugawa's breastplate. Tokugawa took a quick step back and glanced down at his sigil which now had a deep cut across its center. Kenji took his moment and rushed to close the distance, but Tokugawa was not fazed. He locked swords with Kenji and the pair clenched the muscles in their shoulders to come to a standstill. Kenji looked back at Tokugawa; the only things separating them now were the thin blades between their chests. The duo pushed off hard, both stepping back and readying themselves once more. Kenji tightened his grip and raised his sword back up, trying to anticipate Tokugawa's next move. The two men began stepping around the center of the courtyard, watching each other's feet for any sudden moves. As they rotated, the courtyard was illuminated by a moon that had finally broken free of the clouds. Moving at the same time, Kenji and Tokugawa rushed in and exchanged multiple strikes above their heads, each one being blocked by their opponent, before backing off once more. Kenji was breathing heavy, but started to slow down and control his breathing when he realized Tokugawa seemed fine with this level of exertion. Letting Tokugawa make the next move, Kenji stepped closer now trying to bait a strike out of him. Tokugawa took the bait and lunged forward, jabbing out toward Kenji's stomach. Kenji parried the strike off to the right and struck upward toward Tokugawa's shoulder. Letting the attack glance off his armour Tokugawa moved his shoulder back to absorb the blow, and brought his sword back, slashing it across the side of Kenji's right arm. Kenji stepped back and turned his good shoulder toward Tokugawa as his other began to heat up and blood started to seep through his clothes. Tokugawa took his chance and swung for Kenji's neck. Kenji bent his back and ducked underneath, sliding behind Tokugawa. As he got behind him, Kenji struck his sword back and connected with the inside of Tokugawa's knee which sent him stumbling forward to regain his stance. Kenji spun quickly trying not to let his guard down as Tokugawa turned back and stabilized himself. Tokugawa clenched his jaw and tightened his grip. Kenji saw his opponent was getting frustrated with the fight but still knew he could not get over confident. The city was silent as once more the pair circled around the courtyard waiting for their opponent's next strike. Kenji and Tokugawa moved in unison, rushing toward each other with one goal in mind, and then the silent courtyard was filled with the collective gasp of the crowd.

CHAPTER 17

Aiko rubbed her eyes and rolled over, trying unsuccessfully to fall back asleep. But this time as she rubbed the sleep from her eyes, she saw rays of light pierce through the entrance to the cave. Her many attempts at sleep had failed. She sat up against the rock wall and could not stop herself from letting out a big yawn, taking in a large gasp of air. She looked around the cave to see if anyone else had gotten up yet, but no one had. Everyone had a long day yesterday and was sound asleep around her. After grabbing her hand and extending her arms out in front of her to stretch them out she crawled over to Maku and poked him in the shoulder. Maku moved his shoulder and shook his head before his eyes shot open.

"Aiko, what is it? Are you alright?" Maku whispered.

"Yes, I'm fine; it's time to go, the sun is up." Aiko said with a hint of impatience.

"Oh yes, alright. Help me get everyone up." Maku said rubbing his face.

Aiko did as she was told and used the same poke in the shoulder strategy she used on Maku. She got a mixed response. After waking up the last of the group members, Maku and Aiko were the first out of the cave. Maku began picking up supplies and loading them onto Strider as the others began to emerge from the cave. Watching the others begin to pack everything into the few bags they had, she walked over to the pond and sat next to the water. She clenched her toes at the initial chill of the water but soon submerged both her feet. She began to splash the water to the other side of the pond while she waited for the grownups to finish getting ready. Trying to find any animals in the water Aiko bent over and surveyed the floor of the pond.

"Ah!" Aiko let out a gasp.

A small green frog had jumped out of the weeds and landed next her, croaking while it looked up at her, Aiko waved hello to her visitor. She watched as the amphibian hopped past her and into a new set of weeds to once more disappear. She continued to kick her feet in the water as the other kids ran past trying to tag each other. Jun stopped behind her and walked over.

"Want to come and play while we wait for the grownups?" Jun asked.

"No thanks, I'm going to stay here till we leave." Aiko responded.

"Okay. See you later!" Jun rushed off in search of Kin and Etsu.

Aiko sat on her own a while longer before hearing commotion over by the edge of the forest. She got up and walked over to see Maku out front with Hanako by his side addressing the group. The group had formed a semi-circle around the two of them.

"Alright, we are about to head out. Remember to stay close and keep your eyes out while we travel." Maku announced.

"We will let the kids and Nami and Saburo take turns riding Strider as they get tired and we will make it as far as we can before stopping to camp overnight come sun down," Hanako said.

"Are we ready to go?" Maku asked the crowd.

The group gave a collective nod and Maku and Hanako turned to lead the others out of the forest. Aiko ran up beside Hanako and walked close to her leg at the front of the group just behind Maku. As they left the clearing Aiko gave one last hopeful look out toward the direction of the city but was disappointed to see nothing. As she walked Aiko looked around for other creatures who might be following them on their path. She could see squirrels run across the forest floor trying to find food to store before the winter hit. One such animal ran across their path and up the trunk of a tree. Aiko tried to follow it with her gaze but it disappeared at the top of the tree and into the crimson leaves. She began to kick up leaves on the path as the group walked, enjoying the crackling sound they made as they broke.

"Did you want to ride on Strider?" Hanako looked down and asked Aiko.

"No, I can walk."

"Alright, let me know if you get tired."

"Okay."

"You know I used to sneak out to the clearing when I was a child. That's how I knew where it was," Hanako said, trying to change the subject.

"Would not you get in trouble?" Aiko asked.

"Only if I was caught afterwards. Sometimes my parents would get mad but my mother took it better than my father."

"I like exploring too but I never got to do it much. My…" Aiko paused to look at her feet. "My mother usually had me stay inside the walls. She said it was safer."

"That's what my father said too. But I used to go out more once I found the cave."

"That must have been fun," Aiko said looking forward again as she walked.

"Yes, I hid in there all night once from the guards after they came looking for me. Even my mother wasn't very happy then."

Aiko smiled.

"It was a good idea you had about going to Nagoya."

"It was Kenji's idea."

"What do you mean? I saw you whisper to him, wasn't that what you said?"

"Yes, I just didn't want to have to tell everyone."

"Why not? You had the only good idea that night if you ask me." Hanako patted Aiko on the shoulder.

"Well, everyone seemed really angry; especially Jiro and I didn't want him to yell at me."

"He was just upset over what happened, he would not have gotten mad at you."

"I know Kenji would have protected me just like he did for Maku."

"That's right. But I wish Jiro hadn't threatened anyone."

"It's okay. I'm glad Kenji taught him a lesson." Aiko said as she looked ahead of them.

Hanako looked down toward Aiko.

"Kenji resolved the problem but it's not good that someone got hurt."

"But he deserved it after what he said about Kane and my mother."

"Aiko..."

"Do you like Kenji?" Aiko cut her off.

"He is a nice man if 's what you mean."

"But do you want to marry him?" Aiko questioned.

"That's grown up stuff." Hanako laughed.

"You sure seem to smile a lot around him."

"He makes me happy but marriage is not something on my mind lately."

"I don't believe you." Aiko said confidently.

"You are pretty perceptive for a kid, you know that?" Hanako smiled.

"What does that mean?"

"Perceptive? Like, you are good at seeing things that aren't always easy to see. You're a smart kid."

"Thanks, I like looking for things and I love treasure hunts. My father used to hide my birthday presents somewhere in our house and give me clues on how to find them."

"I bet you were very good at them."

"I was." Aiko beamed.

The group had arrived at a large tree and Maku stopped to survey the woods around them. Following suit, the party waited for Maku to finish looking before he turned to face everyone. He told everyone they would rest here for a moment before continuing on toward Nagoya. Aiko was too busy staring at the tree they had stopped at to listen to the rest of what he had to say. The tree stood out from the others because of how big it was. The trunk was much wider and the branches spread out across a much larger area then the ones around it. She looked up to the top and noticed that even though it was bigger at first it did not go as high as the other trees she could see. As everyone else leaned against trees or sat in the grass Aiko walked over to a low branch and jumped up wrapping her arms around it. She swung her legs back and forth to gain enough momentum before swinging her legs around it as well. As she clung to the branch she hung her head upside down letting her hair obstruct her vision. Hanako walked over to her, parted her hair, and then was greeted by an upside down smile.

"Need some help getting on top?" Hanako held out her hands to offer.

"Nope." Aiko shimmied around the branch until she could lift herself to a sitting position.

"Be careful up there, I would not want you to fall."

"I won't."

Aiko shifted over until she could lean her shoulder against the trunk of the tree and dangled her legs off the side of the branch. She watched the group members as they carried on small conversations or stretched parts of their bodies while Maku continued to look out into the forest. After a short while, Maku called out to the group that they were moving on, and Aiko jumped down from the tree, landing with her knees bent to absorb the impact. She ran her fingers through her hair to make sure no leaves or twigs had gotten stuck in it and ran back up to the front of the group. The sun had made its way to the top of the sky and Aiko put her hand above her head to shelter her eyes from it whenever it managed to push past the treetops and into her face. Trying not to worry about the sun, she listened to a conversation between Maku and Saburo who had caught up to walk beside him.

"Have you ever been to Nagoya?" Maku asked Saburo.

"Only a couple of times when I was younger. My father was a fisherman so you can imagine he wasn't too pleased when I became a woodworker and didn't follow in his footsteps."

"Do you think this is the right move for us?"

"I still don't like the idea of leaving my home behind but you made a good point around the fire last night. And besides I have my tools back and my family with me so I'll be fine."

"I just hope the others are as positive as you."

"Oh, I'm sure they will come around, you just have to give them time."

"I hope you're right."

Aiko got bored of their conversation and turned her attention back to her feet to watch the leaves spray up in front of her as she kicked them aside. Her mind drifted to the port city of Nagoya which she only remembered vaguely from her handful of times going there. The city was located on the edge of Japan with its docks always teeming with ships. She could remember the noise of people rushing back and forth and the sounds of ships coming in to dock. One thing that stuck with her was the smell, and the memory of it caused her nose to retract. Aiko never really liked going through the city but she enjoyed when she got to the dock because it meant she got to ride on her father's ship. She liked the ocean and how open it felt. Her father's ship was not the biggest one there but she liked that she could run from one end to the other without getting tired. She recalled standing with her father at the front of the ship and listening to him telling her about all the types of fish swimming under them as they moved across the water. She liked her father's stories but was sad she could not remember details of them. She frowned and continued to walk, trying to think of the details of some of their trips together. Without any luck, Aiko kicked hard at the ground sending a stick that was hiding under the leaves soaring into a tree along their path. She quickly looked around to the others who did not seem to mind her abuse of the stick. She giggled to herself as the party moved on through the forest.

Maku's eyes were scanning the forest and his chin was held high but Aiko could see his shoulders had begun to sag, showing he was not immune to exhaustion. Aiko's shoulders did not feel tired but her feet had begun to get sore and she started to drag them along the ground rather than lift them with each step. She rubbed her eyes that were now struggling to stay open and she could feel the effects of her lack of sleep from the previous night. To her relief, Maku held up his hand and the group came to a stop behind him. He turned to address everyone.

"It's starting to get late and I know we are all tired. This is where we will stop for the night and we'll continue on in the morning."

Everyone nodded their heads in agreement.

"We need people to gather things for a fire and others to come with me and see if we can find some extra food in the forest before nightfall."

"I can start handing out some of the food we have left." Hanako offered.

"Perfect. Afterwards we will decide who wants to take first watch, but for now rest up as much as you can."

Everyone started to disperse to complete their tasks after Maku's speech. Aiko walked over to Maku who was inspecting the arrows in his quiver.

"Can I come with you?" Aiko asked.

"Don't you need to rest? We have been walking for a long time."

"Resting sounds boring. I want to go on a walk with you." Aiko pleaded.

"I'm not going for a walk. Me and some of the others are going to go out and get us some food."

"So why can't I come?"

"Aiko maybe another time, but you should take a break or if you want to help maybe you could join Hanako and hand out some of the remaining food."

"Okay."

Maku put his hand on Aiko's shoulder.

"I'm glad you want to help. You're a good kid."

"Uh huh." Aiko turned to go and find Hanako.

Hanako was busy unpacking some of the food. Aiko walked over and held out her hands.

"Can I help?" She offered.

"Oh sure, that would be great. Thanks Aiko." Hanako gave a smile as she handed Aiko some food.

"I just give some to everyone?"

"Yes, and make sure to come back and get some for yourself."

"Okay." Aiko walked off.

The task was not as exciting as she had hoped for, but at least it was something. She moved from member to member receiving compliments as she went. Most people began eating before Aiko had turned away and some were almost finished by the time she got to the next person. All the other members of the group seemed really hungry and exhausted, but Aiko did her best not to let her energy level affect her mood. She had too many other emotions running through her head to let tiredness get her down. Aiko diligently handed out all of the food to the others within their new camp and went back to receive her share from Hanako. She got her food and took a seat by the fire pit being put together and started to eat. As she ate, she wiggled her toes, they were sore from the trip but she did not want to admit it. She sat cross legged in an attempt to ignore them. Aiko munched on a handful of berries as Jun came and sat down beside her. She sighed and continued to look into the fire pit that had yet to create a flame for Saburo who had been stoking it.

"How are you Aiko?" Jun asked.

"Fine."

"That was a long walk hey? My feet are sore."

"We still have a long way to go tomorrow." Aiko responded.

"Are you tired yet? Lots of the others are tired but I'm not ready for bed yet."

"Not really, but I've had trouble sleeping anyway." Aiko admitted.

"Why? Do you have nightmares? I hate having nightmares."

Aiko did not answer, putting more food into her mouth.

"Have you ever been to this place we are going to?"

"Yes, but not for a while."

"Wasn't it your idea to go to there?"

"I used to go there with my father; he has a small ship docked there."

"That's so cool! I've never been on a ship. What's it like?" Jun was intrigued.

"Well, it can get really windy if you get out into open water and sometimes it's hard to stay on your feet."

"Did you ever get seasick? I heard you can throw up from being on a boat."

"I never did but my father said he did when he first went out on the water."

"Ew, that must have been gross." Jun recoiled from the thought.

"I just hope Kazuo is still there."

"Who's Kazuo?"

"He's a dockworker who always went out with me and my father. He would normally control the ship so my father could stand out on the deck with me and my mother." Aiko paused and dropped her shoulders.

"Ah ha!" Saburo clapped as the wood in the fire pit was finally set ablaze.

"Yay!" Jun cheered along with him.

Others began to gather around the fire as they realized it had been lit. Aiko stuck her hands out toward it just as many of the others did. She could feel the warmth hitting her palms as it started emanating from the flames. She did not realize she could hardly feel her finger tips until the heat began to reach them. Soon everyone had gathered around the fire and began talking about different subjects Aiko was not interested in. After finishing her food, she walked out to look in the direction Maku had left in. To her disappointment all she could see was a dark empty forest. Most of the creatures had already tucked themselves away for the night with only a few scurrying across the ground trying to find a spot to rest. Aiko started to turn back toward the fire before seeing something in the woods that made her stop. It looked small and thin and quickly she realized it was coming right at her. The arrow pierced the bark of the tree next to her causing her to jump in fear.

"Aiko, watch out!" Maku was running toward her followed closely by Isas.

Aiko darted behind the trunk of a nearby tree and crouched down. Isas ran toward where the arrow had been fired and tackled an archer who had positioned himself behind a bush. Aiko tried to see what was happening but the fight was being obscured by the foliage.

"Ambush!" A voice shouted behind her.

The members of the group that had the remaining swords formed a circle around the fire, and Aiko saw her chance to run back to them. She rushed into the circle that had formed, and stuck close to Hanako. Her eyes scanned around her but could not see anything past the trees. Isas and Maku ran into the circle. Aiko could see Isas' knuckles had smears of blood covering them.

"Stay close to one another! Keep your eyes open!" Maku commanded.

The group tightened their formation and stared back out at the forest unsure of where the next attack would come from. Aiko heard a swoosh of air rush past her followed by a cry of pain. She turned to look and saw Jiro collapsed on the grass, an arrow stuck imbedded in his shoulder. Aiko gasped and looked away.

"Where are they?" She asked.

"We cannot just stay here!" Hanako said.

"Just stick close." Maku tried to reassure the group.

The terrified party started to move slowly keeping a tight circle around their injured friend. Suddenly another cry was let out, from the direction of the forest. Aiko squinted to try and see the source of the sound. As she looked into the trees another yell was let out, this time from behind them causing her to turn again.

"They're picking us off! Attack!" A command was shouted from the trees.

Soldiers sprung from the shadows and charged toward the group. Maku had first contact and jabbed his sword out, piercing the man's abdomen and swiftly kicking him off to prepare for another opponent. A second soldier ran at the group but was met by the angry hooves of Strider, whose legs connected with the man, sending him crashing down to the grass. Four more soldiers ran toward the group on Aiko's side and Aiko clung to Hanako's leg. Before the first soldier could reach her, Aiko watched as he collapsed to the ground at her feet. He laid there with a large dent in his skull and she knelt down to pick up a rock that had landed there. The remaining soldiers stopped and turned around trying to determine where the projectile had come from. Aiko looked up as two swords were drawn, and Kenji walked out of the shadows. The soldiers readied themselves and all charged at once. Kenji deflected the first attack off to his left and followed with a forceful slash across the soldier's chest. He repositioned himself to face the next man, who had foolishly gone for an overhead attack with both arms raised above his head. Kenji gave him a swift kick to the chest causing him to stumble back into his comrade, and Kenji slashed with both his swords across the man's breastplate, causing the man to fall to the grass. The last soldier let out a battle cry, cut short by both of Kenji's swords piercing his abdomen. Aiko watched as the soldier's body went limp and was soon only held up by Kenji's swords. Kenji pulled back hard, removing his weapons from the soldier's abdomen so he too could lay lifeless next to the others. Kenji wiped both his swords on his pants and placed them on his back. Aiko noticed his breathing was heavy but regardless she ran out of the tight group and wrapped her arms around him. Kenji eyes went wide and he put one arm around Aiko's back.

"You have some explaining to do, my boy." Saburo said.

"What happened to Jiro?" Kenji refocused on Jiro who was now sitting up and clutching his shoulder.

"Struck by an arrow. He'll be fine but it'll be sore for the trip." Hanako said as she inspected his injury without looking up.

"You were just too slow." Maku smiled as he approached and embraced his friend.

"Aside from Jiro, is everyone alright?" Kenji asked.

"I think so, just shocked is all." Isas replied.

"Well, let's try and get some sleep before we leave again."

"Not before you tell us what happened." Maku argued.

"Alright, it's not an exciting story."

As Hanako began her work on removing the arrow from Jiro's shoulder the group gathered around the fire and waited in anticipation for the story that was going to be told. Aiko took a seat right beside Kenji and looked up at him eagerly awaiting what he was going to say.

“I’m sorry I didn’t tell all of you but I left to try and buy you as much time as possible.” Kenji began.

“Then how did they get here before you?” Questioned Hanako’s mother.

“They must have sent out a scouting party right before I left the city.”

“You went back inside? You’re crazier than I thought.” Jiro said trying not to focus on his injury.

“I went to see Tokugawa. I knew he would not refuse a duel with me in front of his soldiers and I thought it would be the best way to distract the most people at once.”

“You fought him?” Aiko said amazed.

“Yes. I have admittedly gained a small amount of respect for him, at least from a warrior’s perspective. He held nothing back.” Kenji stared into the fire as he recalled his duel.

The crowd around the courtyard let out a gasp as Kenji and Tokugawa slashed simultaneously at each other’s necks. Both men had to bend backwards to avoid the fatal strike and spun quickly once again to face one another. Kenji’s breathing was heavy and he was having trouble hiding it. He knew he could not win this fight if it kept up like this, but he could not think of a way out. His only goal was to keep the fight going as long as possible so his group could make as much distance as they could. Tokugawa could see Kenji’s stance begin to falter and he knew he had the upper hand. Kenji could see the confidence spread over his face and hoped he could use this to his advantage. Kenji lowered his sword slightly hoping to bait an attack out of his opponent. Tokugawa took his opportunity and rushed at Kenji, swinging his sword down across his chest. Kenji sidestepped the strike and let go of his sword with one hand to strike Tokugawa across the face with a palm strike. Taken by surprise Tokugawa stumbled forward before turning to face him, his eyes so angered Kenji thought flames may burst out. Kenji had taken the honour out of this duel by hitting Tokugawa and both he and the crowd knew it. Now Kenji waited to see how Tokugawa would react. The rules of the duel had changed and now it was up to Tokugawa to decide what to do. Tokugawa looked Kenji in the eyes and sheathed his sword. Kenji's eyes went wide but he did the same. The fight had come to an end. Kenji slowly walked toward Tokugawa, hoping he could buy even more time for his travelling group. As Kenji walked up to Tokugawa, he noticed a slight bend in his knees. He tried to step back but it was too late. Tokugawa spun around and switched his feet shooting out a back kick directly into Kenji's sternum. Toppling to the ground, Kenji exhaled sharply and struggled to regain breath. The wind had been knocked out of him and Tokugawa stood towering over him. A hush settled over the crowd as Tokugawa crossed his arms in front of his chest. Kenji sat up and put one had back to stabilize and the other up on his knee in hopes of more protection.

"You should go save your friends, we're done here." Tokugawa said before turning to leave the courtyard.

Kenji stood up quickly and stared at Tokugawa's back surprised and relieved he had not had his life ended right then and there. *What did he mean about my friends? He knew?* Kenji gave a quick glance at the people around him who were still frozen to their spots before running out of Sekigahara and toward the forest.

Kenji looked up from the fire and around at the other group members who were staring back at him. No one spoke a word but Kenji could see by their expressions they were not expecting the end of his story.

"So, he just let you go?" Hanako said busy wrapping up Jiro's shoulder.

"I was trying to buy you all as much time as I could, but I guess he knew already. Being honourable, he could not decline the duel but he was also distracting me."

"So, if they are on to us is it still safe to go to Nagoya?" Isas asked.

"We're close enough now that anyone else he sends out after us will not get there before we do. So as long as we keep a low profile in the city, we should still be okay." Kenji said.

"You got here just in time, glad to have you back, friend." Maku said with a smile.

Kenji nodded.

"Time to get some sleep, and then continue the journey tomorrow?" Kenji asked.

"Yes, I think we will need all the energy we can get for tomorrow." Saburo agreed.

"Okay, you all can rest and I'll stay up for watch." Kenji offered.

"Are you sure?" Maku questioned.

"Yes, I will be fine; you have all had a long day."

Seeing Kenji's mind was made up, the group began getting up and settling into their own spots on the grass. Jiro rolled over to try and take the pain away from his injury and Hanako got comfortable next to her mother. Maku gave a friendly salute to Kenji before lying down with the rest of the group and Kenji picked up a stick next to him to begin stoking the fire. He pushed over a log in an attempt to keep the fire alive but it did not seem to help much. He turned to get up and retrieve a new one when he was met with a bloodied rock inches from his face.

"I got you your rock back. In case you wanted to keep it." Aiko said with a smile.

Kenji grinned and took the rock from her hand placing it down by his feet.

"I would prefer to not, but thank you anyway." Kenji said. "How has the trip been?"

"Before we got attacked you mean?" Aiko took a seat beside Kenji.

"Yes, before you got attacked." Kenji smiled again.

"It was alright, really boring mostly. I did get to climb a tree when we took a break."

"That sounds fun; did you get to the top?"

"No, but I could have. I didn't want to worry Hanako. She was already nervous after one branch."

"Oh, I see. She just doesn't want you to get hurt."

"Yes, I know, but I can take care of myself."

"I'm sure you can. But why aren't you in bed?"

"I'm not tired." Aiko grabbed another stick to pick up where Kenji left off. "And I kinda have trouble sleeping now." She admitted.

"I know what 's like, but it'll pass eventually, I promise."

"So why are your two swords different?" Aiko asked changing the subject.

"Because I got them at different times."

"I like the one with the red handle and the dragon on it." Aiko admired the short sword hung on his back.

"I do too. Apparently, it was my father's. He used it when he was a soldier and had planned on giving it to me anyway."

"What about the other one?"

"This one I got afterward with my uncle. We were travelling together and I found it. It was in pretty good condition, so I kept it."

"You mean you killed someone for it?" Aiko questioned.

Kenji sighed, remembering it was hard to get things past this girl.

"Yes, I did. He was the first person I had ever killed."

The pair was interrupted by the call of a bird in the treetops above them. Aiko's eyes shot up trying to search for the animal but it was hidden away in the leaves. Aiko shrugged and focused back on Kenji.

"How old were you? Why did you do it?" Aiko asked filled with curiosity.

"I was travelling with my uncle and we got attacked on the road. I had to defend myself so I did what my uncle had taught me. I was fourteen."

"Was it hard?"

"At the time I didn't really notice it but I thought about it for a while afterwards."

"Do you think about it now? The people you've killed."

Kenji exhaled. Aiko was bombarding him with tougher questions than he was ready for.

"Every now and again, yes. I try not to get distracted by it."

Aiko tossed her stick in the fire and leaned against Kenji's chest. Looking down Kenji saw she was staring back into the flames which had engulfed the stick she had tossed.

"I still think about mother. I think that's why I have a hard time sleeping."

"It'll get better Aiko, but these things take time. Sleeping will become easier."

Kenji put his arm around Aiko and she reacted by curling in closer to his chest.

"I always felt safe when she was around, but now I get scared over dumb things."

"It's natural to be scared, and it's okay." Kenji said trying to comfort Aiko.

"Do you…" Aiko paused to succumb to a yawn. "Do you get scared?"

"Of course. I just know I can overcome my fears so that helps a bit."

Kenji took a deep breath in before exhaling.

"You know you'll be safe with me, right?"

Kenji looked down at Aiko who had closed her eyes and was breathing slowly on his chest. He smiled and turned to bend over and pick her up. Holding Aiko in his arms he carried her toward where the others slept and kneeling down Kenji placed Aiko down on the grass and turned to walk back toward the fire.

"I know." Aiko said from the grass.

Kenji smiled to himself once again as he sat back next to the fire as it illuminated the night.

CHAPTER 18

The night had been uneventful after his chat with Aiko, with only a few sounds muttered from the surrounding wildlife to fill the emptiness of the forest. Kenji stood and stretched his shoulders while kicking at the fire that was trying to cling to life. He gave it one last stomp, turning his heel in the embers to ensure its attempts failed. The shadows of the night had begun to give way to bright rays of sun trying to get past the canopy above and onto the forest floor. The rustling of bodies could be heard behind him, but when he turned, he saw the group still fast asleep on the ground. He moved toward them ready to get them moving again but was cut off by Strider who had trotted up and was now blocking his path.

"Hey, friend." Kenji gave Strider a pat on the neck.

Strider huffed a puff of air into Kenji's face.

"I'm sorry I didn't come and say hello to you first." Kenji said, as if he knew his mount was mad at him.

Strider trotted off to go and find some breakfast before the trip ahead, and Kenji resumed his task of waking everyone. He walked over to Maku first and gave him a nudge with his foot, trying to wake him. Maku rolled over, ignoring Kenji's attempts. Next Kenji tried giving Maku a firm kick to his side which caused his eyes to shoot open before rolling back over to face him.

"I'm ready." Maku said, trying not to sound groggy.

"Sure you are. Help me get the others up." Kenji smirked.

Maku slowly and steadily got to his feet to help Kenji in waking the other members of the group. One by one, everyone began getting up and stretching various limbs before gathering anything left on the ground. Afterward, everyone gathered around the charcoal remains of the fire and awaited instruction. Maku took Strider's reins and lead him up beside the group while Kenji walked out in front of them. He stared back at bodies that tried to look awake but whose eyes betrayed them. Tightening the swords on his back, Kenji looked around at the others before turning and raising his hand.

"Time to go." Kenji said with as much enthusiasm as he could muster.

Gradually the group fell in line with him, and started the remainder of their walk toward Nagoya. The morning air was cooler than he had thought it would be and Kenji found himself rubbing his hands together within a couple minutes of the walk. Despite his hands being slightly cold Kenji enjoyed the fall season. All of the colours gave a vibrancy to his surroundings and the brisk air kept him awake and his senses heightened. As the group walked, their path was intermittently being cut off by passing wildlife vying for a chance to stock up on food for the coming winter. The children in the group wasted no time in creating a game out of all the creatures who ran around them and began competing to see who could spot the most during their trip. Not interested in the game, Aiko ran up beside Kenji and walked close to his leg. Kenji smiled as she approached and got a smile in return.

"So, have you ever been to Nagoya?" Maku asked having come up alongside them.

"No, I haven't. I don't know much about it either."

"Apparently it's a port city and its size has grown quite a bit in recent years, probably due to the increase in trade."

"Hopefully we can use that to blend in. I don't want to attract too much attention."

"It might be hard with a group of this size. Do we even know what we are going to say?"

"I haven't really thought about that yet."

"My parents' friend in the city is really nice, I'm sure he'll help us out." Aiko chimed in.

"He does sound like our best bet." Maku added.

"Regardless, when we get there, we should try to keep to ourselves, and try not to talk to anyone we don't have to."

"Agreed. Can you believe after all this we are actually going to leave?"

"I thought this was your idea?" Kenji questioned.

"It was, but just thinking about it the last couple of days I cannot believe it. I just assumed I would always live in Japan."

"So did I. But like you said, I don't really see a better option. There is not much left for any of us here."

"I'm sure we'll find a better spot for us to go, maybe one of the smaller islands off the coast where we can settle down."

"Perhaps. First priority is keeping these people safe."

"You've done a great job of it so far."

"Yes!" Aiko agreed.

"I just want to get everyone on a ship and then I can rest easy." Kenji said.

"We'll make it. We've made it this far already."

"I admire your positivity."

"It's my best trait." Maku said with a playful shrug.

The pair shared a laugh before Maku departed to the back of the pack.

"I'm going to check in and make sure everyone is doing alright."

"Sure thing." Kenji waved.

Kenji looked down at Aiko who was twiddling her thumbs as they walked.

"Are you excited to go back to Nagoya?"

"I guess so. I like the ocean but the city is crowded. There are so many people all over the place and it smells bad sometimes." Aiko scrunched her nose.

"You did really good coming up with this idea for us. I'm proud of you."

Aiko grinned.

"You know you are going to have to teach me about ships. I've never been on one before."

"Really?"

"No never. You'll have to give me the tour."

"Okay!" Aiko beamed. "It's really fun but you have to be good at balance cause sometimes the ship will rock in the water."

"Then you'll have to catch me." Kenji grinned.

"No way! You're way too heavy." Aiko retorted.

"Gee thanks." Kenji said with a smirk.

"Oh, you know what I mean. You're bigger than me."

"I'm just teasing you." Kenji said patting her on the shoulder. "Do you think we should rest up here? Are you tired?"

"I'm not, but some of them might need to." Aiko laughed.

"Let's take a break up here then."

Kenji held up his hand to signal a stop and the group came to a halt.

"We are going to rest here for a moment before continuing on. Try to ration out any remaining food evenly." Kenji announced.

Everyone spread out slightly with most taking a seat in the grass to stretch their legs. Aiko quickly looked to see if there was a tree she could climb and Maku began to run out ahead and Kenji assumed it was to scout. Kenji walked over to Jiro who was sitting up against the trunk of a tree rubbing his shoulder.

"How's the arm?" Kenji asked.

"It hurts, but Hanako said I'll be fine once it heals."

"I'm glad to hear it. I guess I'll make you carry any wood we find from now on."

"Ha ha." Jiro laughed sarcastically.

"Look I'm sorry about what happened back at the cave. I overreacted."

"No, you didn't. I was being too emotional and I took it too far. In hindsight, I'm glad you put me in my place."

"So, are we good?" Kenji asked trying not to sound too hopeful.

"Yes, of course. We all need to work together now if we're going to make it."

"I'm glad we agree. You rest up that shoulder and I'm going to check on the others."

"Alright."

Kenji sighed, glad he had not made an enemy in the group. He already had enough on his mind.

Stretching his arms up over his head, Kenji went to see Hanako who had handed out what remained of the food. She smiled as he approached and began to separate some berries for him.

"Hungry?" Hanako asked.

"Practically all the time, it's a constant struggle." Kenji responded with a grin.

"Hopefully we'll get some food from the city somehow because we are beginning to run out." Hanako warned handing Kenji the berries.

Kenji ate some of the berries before responding.

"When we get there, we may have to split up to gather supplies. I told Maku I didn't want to, but we may not have much of a choice."

"I hope Aiko's friend can really help us. It could be dead end."

"I don't think Aiko would have brought it up if she didn't think he would help."

"I know, I'm just worried."

"Yes, we all are. But you have been a big help to this group. You've been great support to them." Kenji said trying to reassure her.

"We help them together. My part in it is small."

"Don't sell yourself short. You have done a great job."

"Thank you, Kenji." Hanako blushed.

"So, you think we will be ready to move out soon?"

"Yes, I think so. Do you know how long it is until we reach the city?"

"I have a rough idea from talking to Aiko about it, but I believe Maku ran out to check the path ahead. Maybe he'll see something."

"Should I tell everyone to get ready to move again?"

"Yes, we'll start walking again once Maku's back. Thanks, Hanako." Kenji reached out and touched her shoulder, to which she smiled.

As Kenji walked away, he looked out in the trees ahead of the group trying to eye where Maku was. Without any luck, he started formulating a plan of what to do once they hit the city. A group of their size would certainly attract attention, and at the very least get people talking. He knew he could not announce they were refugees because if he remembered correctly, Ichiro had told him Nagoya was where Tokugawa was originally based. He would have to find a way to get his group through the city without arousing the suspicion of the guards. And there was the matter of obtaining supplies they would need for the journey, while hoping Tokugawa's men did not catch up to them. He could see why Hanako was worried, but he tried to think of the positives and focus on what they could do. As everyone began standing and preparing to leave again, Maku jogged back to the group slightly out of breath.

"How far did you run?" Kenji asked a tired Maku.

"I was just trying to see if the way was clear but I saw something else." Maku paused to regain some more breath.

"We must be getting close because I found a road not too far from here."

"Great work. That's sure to lift the group's spirits a bit."

"We are going to walk the rest of the way, right?" Maku asked.

"Yes 's the plan. Want to ride on Strider on the way there?" Kenji laughed.

"No, no, I'm good. Just a few more seconds and I'll be fine."

Kenji shook his head and turned to face the patient crowd.

"Okay everyone, Maku found a road up ahead which means we should be getting close. Hopefully we'll get there before sundown," he announced.

Aiko leapt from the branch of a tree to rejoin Kenji who had once again started to lead the group forward toward the port city of Nagoya.

CHAPTER 19

Just as Maku had said, they were close to a road. Only a short while after restarting their trip the group came across an opening in the forest that gave way to a fairly wide road. Sighs of relief could be heard from the party once they walked onto the road, happy they could see the first signs of the city. Kenji was more concerned about the possibility of an ambush on an open road like this, and kept his eyes scanning the trees that surrounded them. He looked to Maku who did the same, but held his hand near the hilt of his sword as they continued forward. They had both experienced the dangers of the world long enough that they knew they could not let their guard down. The group travelled the road until they came upon a sign off the side of the trail. NAGOYA-SAKI, Nagoya ahead. Kenji smiled as they passed it as did many others of the group. Walking farther down the path a gust of wind met the group head on and Kenji could smell water travelling along it.

"We must be close now." Hanako said happily.

As the travelling group got closer to the city, Kenji started to hear the sounds of people working and the crashing of water on rocks. Soon afterward, the forest gave way to a sprawling patch of flat grass acting as a natural welcome mat in front of the city of Nagoya. The walls were not as high as those at Sekigahara, but were littered with the same uniformed guards patrolling the tops. Two sentries stood watch at the gate but had not noticed the group emerge from the forest. The defining feature of the city was the castle that stood proudly inside its walls. Kenji could only see the top half over the walls, but its grand ornate design was still evident from where he stood. He could not marvel at the sight of it for too long though, and quickly turned back to face his group.

"Let's find a spot to stay inside the trees for now. The guards haven't noticed us yet."

The group did as they were told and dispersed back into the treeline.

"Why are we hiding, Kenji?" Riku asked.

"We don't know how they'll respond to a group this big. I think it's best if a few of us go in at first. Maybe try and find Aiko's friend."

"So, we just wait here until you come back for us?" Isas asked.

"We will not take long. Once we know a group this big will not be a problem someone will come back to let everyone else in."

"Why don't we just go in smaller groups or pairs but separately, so we don't raise suspicion?" Naoko suggested.

"We need somewhere to meet once we are all inside." Maku said.

"How about the in the market place? If I remember there should be one close to the center of the city near the docks." Saburo said.

"Then there's our plan. Aiko, Saburo, Hanako and I will go first with Strider and see if we can find out where Aiko's friend is. Jiro and Riku try and find out how and where we can get some supplies and the rest of you go in pairs and take what we have left. After we're in, we meet at the market. Clear?"

Everyone nodded in agreement. Saburo led Strider over before letting Aiko and Hanako hop on. The group walked out toward the entrance of the city and were met with the stares of the sentries.

"Hold a moment. What's the reason for coming to Nagoya?" One guard questioned.

Before Kenji could answer Saburo stepped forward to answer the guard's question.

"Hello sir. My son and his wife and I are here taking a trip. My granddaughter has always wanted to see the famous castle built here and we were hoping we could go to see it." Saburo motioned to Aiko who sat with Hanako atop Strider.

The man eyed Kenji up and down before glancing toward the others. After a brief visual inspection, the soldier waved his hand behind him motioning for them to move along. As they walked through the main gate Kenji shot a glance at Saburo with a raised eye brow.

"First thing that came to mind." Saburo responded.

Kenji shrugged and the small group moved deeper into the city. They quickly ran into a dense crowd, unbothered that they were trying to get through. A mix of fisherman carrying their haul from their boats, parents walking their children to the shops, and soldiers patrolling the streets were just some of the throng of people panned out in front of them. The scurrying crowds mostly parted around Strider and Saburo who led him, but Kenji was walking out to their side and did his best to dodge incoming people as they tried to get closer to the market. A young man rushed past Kenji, bumping his shoulder and continuing on without a glance. Kenji already did not like this type of environment. He had to crane his neck to peer past the heads of the crowd and spotted what he thought were trader stalls, and pointed toward them for Saburo. Kenji tried not to shove people out of his way but made sure to keep his shoulders firm so as to not get pushed back by anyone passing. The road they were on opened up slightly and began to curve, creating a round center area filled with rows of stalls each with a different assortment of products. Kenji was surprised by the atmosphere of the market, much calmer than the road they had just come from. Here citizens were walking slowly, browsing the selections of goods they could purchase, or were standing still looking around. The main difference now was the noise. As opposed to the main street, the market was filled with the sounds of supplies being moved and people shouting out pricing for their stands, each one trying to yell louder than their competition to attract customers.

"Rice brought from these very fields!" One stall owner shouted into the crowd.

"Maguro! Fresh maguro!" Another shop owner shouted while holding a large bluefin tuna toward Kenji.

Kenji shook his head rejecting the man's offer of the tuna and the group moved forward through the dense crowd to try and find the docks. It was not hard to find the docks, because as soon as Kenji looked up, he could see the masts of ships reaching into the sky. Small and medium sized ships took up the space at the docks. As they drew closer, the full scent of the ocean was wafted onto the group and Kenji was taken by surprise at the difference of the air near the water. The wooden docks were wide and sturdy but covered in mud and other trash left behind by sailors. Yet the air somehow smelled cleaner than the inner city market. The breeze coming off the top of the water almost caused Kenji to shiver as they walked out onto the docks. Aiko and Hanako got down from Strider and Hanako took hold of the reins.

"I'll stay with Strider if you want to go look for Aiko's friend." Hanako offered.

"And I will make my way back to the market to start looking out for the others as they get through the gate." Saburo suggested.

"Alright, Aiko and I will look around for her friend. Stay close." Kenji looked down at Aiko.

"I know." Aiko replied.

The group split up and Aiko took Kenji's hand to lead him to where she thought her friend might be. She darted in and out of the crowd passing them on the dock and Kenji had to stay on his toes to keep up with her. She led him to a small building off the side of the dock. The door was partially open, and Aiko took it as an invitation to let herself in. The inside was about as big as Kenji would have expected, but it was made to look smaller by the shelves that lined the walls, well stocked with fishing rods, assorted bait and other equipment. A desk was in the center of the shop with another doorway behind it, the contents of the back room obscured from where he stood. Rustling could be heard from the room and Kenji knew the shop was not empty.

"Kazuo are you here? It's me Aiko!" She called into the back room.

"Aiko? What are you doing here? I'll be out in a moment!" A voice called back.

Kenji squinted as if in deep thought. The voice sounded familiar but then again it could have been any man's voice from deep in the shop. He shook his head and took a glance back through the front door.

"Are you okay in here if I go watch outside?" Kenji asked.

"Oh yes, sure. I'll find out where the ship is." Aiko said confidently.

Kenji walked back through the front of the shop to follow what caught his attention. The sounds of creaking wood bellowed through the city as a ship pulled into the dock. Kenji tried not to look like he was impressed when a massive Atakebune came into port, but his mouth fell open slightly nonetheless. Kenji recalled stories told to him by Ichiro of the Atakebune, huge naval war ships stocked to the brim with soldiers ready to board any other vessel they came into contact with. Their colossal size made them ideal for transporting legions of soldiers, usually those who specialized in boarding enemy ships. Despite the size of the Atakebune, they generally were not sturdy enough to house a large number of cannons on their decks, so the soldiers they carried were essential in winning naval battles. On the front of this particular ship was an ornately designed figurehead in the shape of a dragon head, and the flags all bore Tokugawa's symbol. As the warship came to a stop, dockworkers rushed to ensure it was secured properly and to make sure the way was cleared for any soldiers who wished to disembark. Once a path off the ship had been cleared, the surrounding workers stepped back and Kenji could hear boots pounding the ground as legions of soldiers poured out of the ship. They passed Kenji and the other people on the dock without a glance, and Kenji surveyed the types of soldiers marching past him. They were not only regular foot soldiers, but also Yumi archers, Ashigaru musketeers carrying their muskets, and Yamabushi wielding their pikes. They strode across the docks and into the city. Now that Tokugawa had won, it seemed he was fortifying the port city with more reinforcements, which did not bode well for Kenji and his group if they were to be caught. Kenji stood at attention as some of the other citizens did, as the last remaining soldiers passed him, before relaxing his shoulders and watching them split off into the streets.

"Kenji! Come quick!" Saburo was jogging toward him through the soldiers.

"What is it?" Kenji said alarmed by the tone in Saburo's voice.

"It's Jun. He stole some fruit off one of the market stalls and got caught. You need to come sort it out."

"Fine." Kenji gave Saburo a displeased look and the two took off in a jog toward the market centre.

When they arrived, a circular crowd had formed around one of the stalls and Jun was at the middle of it with Hanako and Haru by his side. The rest of Kenji's group had made it into the city and were dispersed within the crowd. Jiro and Naoko were yelling at the stall owner and some displeased customers while

Isas and Fuyu were standing in front of their children next to Hanako's mother. As they got closer, Nami rushed toward them in panic.

"Kenji, you have to do something."

Kenji stepped into the center of the crowd to try and defuse the situation.

"Do you know this kid too? He tried to rob me!" The stall owner yelled at Kenji now.

"Look, it was an honest mistake. He'll return what he took and we'll be on our way." Kenji said while holding his hands in front of him.

"He already took a bite out of it! It's no good to me now!"

"He was just hungry. He will apologize and I'll make sure it doesn't happen again." Kenji spoke in a calm slow tone.

"He needs to be punished for this crime!" The man reached out and grabbed Jun's bicep causing him to yell and to try to wriggle out of his grasp.

Kenji stepped in between them and pushed the man's arm off of Jun before stepping up almost chest to chest with him. The man's body tightened up not wanting to back down but his eyes were nervous betraying his façade. Kenji looked back into the man's eyes and stood firmly in front of him.

"We'll leave you and your stall alone but you will not lay a hand on him." Kenji's tone turned deep and serious. "Good day."

Kenji turned to leave but not before the man grabbed Kenji's left wrist to pull him back. Kenji turned and tightened his fist.

"You should teach him some manners." The owner warned.

Kenji squared up with the man and reached his right hand underneath his left and took hold of the man's thumb before switching his left hand onto the back on the man's hand and twisting his wrist toward the ground. The man yelled in pain as the locking of his joint caused him to drop onto his knee. Kenji held his hands where they were keeping the tension on the man's wrist and stepped up close to him once more.

"I hope you have good luck with your products for the rest of today." Kenji said before releasing his hand.

The stall owner sat on the ground and began rubbing his wrist as Kenji turned to kneel down in front of Jun.

"We'll talk about this later but for now we are all going to go to the docks okay?"

Jun nodded and Kenji stood up once more. Some of the crowd around them had left to continue their day but most had stayed and were looking back at Kenji with a concerned look on their faces. As he walked out of the crowd the rest of his group slowly followed suit and they departed toward the dock together. None of them spoke a word until they got to the edge of the dock and Jun pulled on Kenji's pant leg.

"I'm sorry Kenji. I was just really hungry." Jun frowned.

"I know Jun but it's wrong to steal food. We will find a way to get more food before we leave, I promise."

"Okay." Jun still looked disappointed.

"Now stick close to your mother while we're here okay?"

Jun nodded without looking up. Kenji gave Jun a pat on the shoulder while looking toward Aiko who was running toward them from the shop they entered earlier. She had a grin on her face as she stopped in the middle of everyone.

"My friend said he'd help us. He's getting the ship ready to leave but said we will have to wait until morning cause it's too late now."

"What are we going to do until morning?" Nami asked.

"He said there is an old warehouse that's not far from his shop. One of his friends tries to keep it up, but no one really uses it. We can sleep on the upper level."

"Great work Aiko." Hanako ruffled her hair.

"We can start heading there now and get set up. But where's Maku and Riku?" Kenji asked now realizing they were missing group members.

"Maku took Riku and some of the better quality weapons to try and barter them for food. I told them to meet us by the docks when we got back." Saburo explained.

"Alright, do you mind staying back to watch for them while we see if we can get set up in the warehouse?" Kenji asked.

"Sure, I can."

"Great thanks. We'll send someone back to show you the way once we get there."

"I'll show you where it is. Let's go!" Aiko left happily enjoying how much she was getting to help.

The group laughed in unison as they followed Aiko down the dock.

CHAPTER 20

The warehouse was large and positioned in a rundown part of the shipyard. Most of the higher windows were boarded up or broken and one of the main doors was so cracked it almost acted as another ground floor window. Old piles of supplies were laid out by one of the side entrances and rodents could be seen running across the ground outside. The whole area made it feel like they were in an entirely different city. Kenji led the group to the front entrance and slowly pushed the one main door that was still fully intact. The party was met by the shrill squeaking of rusted hinges being used for the first time in a long while. Upon entering the fairly spacious interior, Kenji noticed most of the ground floor was being taken up by old farming equipment lying dormant. Toward the back of the building there was a large wooden ladder positioned against the rafters that made up the second level. A couple of rungs were broken off but the majority of the ladder looked like it could still serve its purpose. Kenji moved to it and gave some of the bottom rungs a firm push just to make sure. He turned back to look at the group before giving a shrug and grabbing onto the edges of the ladder. He carefully made his way up until he sat on top and gave a reassuring thumbs up to the others below. One by one the remaining group members made their way up to join him and they all stood looking back down to the floor below as if they had conquered a great climb. The second level was mostly empty space with the exception being some old handheld tools lying on two old cobweb filled crates in the far back corner. Gradually everyone began picking their spots among the rafters and sat down for a rest. Kenji positioned himself by one of the upper windows, and put his arm up against its frame. He stared out at the tip of the dock he could see from the warehouse. As the sun gracefully made its way down toward the outlying horizon, the activity on the dock had decreased significantly. Only a couple of men could be seen walking the edge of the docks and a few of the smaller fishing boats had their lanterns on to light the way for late coming fisherman.

"I'll go out to get Saburo and the others before the sun gets too low." Jiro offered.

Kenji nodded in response without taking his eyes from the view out the window. He was fixated on the horizon that looked so far away and yet they had to go out and get to it in order to leave tomorrow. He had never thought about anywhere else but Japan before. He knew there were other places out there from the few times his mother or Ichiro talked about it, but he never planned on getting anywhere close to them. What troubled him was that they still did not know their destination. They had all agreed to leave Japan for a new place they could call home, but none of them knew where that place was. Kenji began to picture what some of the outer islands might be like, and hoped it would someday feel like home, although nothing had felt like home to him since Ikebe had gone up in flames nine years ago. He shook his head to get rid of the picture in his mind. Suddenly a shimmering light shone from beside him causing him to turn his head. Nami had found a lantern and managed to light it up and place it on top of the old crates. He began to sink back into his thoughts of the islands, but was once again distracted by the sound of people entering from the main doors. He looked down to see Jiro followed by Saburo, Riku and Maku carrying a large crate in both arms. Confused, Kenji climbed down the ladder to greet them. Riku carried two sacks in her hands but she seemed to have gotten the easy job compared to Maku who was trying to make it look like the crate he carried was not heavy.

"Need any help with that?" Kenji offered as he came down from the ladder.

"Oh yes, Maku made me carry the heavy things." Riku held out her arms with a smile.

Maku rolled his eyes as Kenji took the sacks from Riku and placed them in an empty spot behind the ladder.

"So how did you manage to get all this? I'm impressed." Kenji remarked.

"You and I are now the only ones who have swords, but I figured we are so close to getting out of here it was better to have supplies." Maku responded.

"We met a merchant who sold all sorts of supplies and he agreed to take our swords in exchange for food and some medical supplies." Riku added.

"Good job to both of you. I'll make sure Hanako gets the first aid supplies sorted out. Let's get the rest stored away for now."

Hanako came down the ladder without being called and started rifling through the crate, sorting out anything that was not food. Kenji looked at what they had brought back and was even more impressed upon closer inspection. An assortment of fruit and vegetables filled one sack and the other had rice and bread inside. Inside the crate, aside from the medical supplies Hanako had separated, were some clothes and several jugs of water. Kenji could not help but smile as he looked through what had been brought back.

"Any word on our way out of here?" Maku asked.

"Aiko met with her friend at the dock and she said the ship will be ready to depart tomorrow. We'll stay the night here and leave once the sun's up."

"That's good to hear. Did you see how many soldiers were dispatched to this city? They are everywhere now."

"Yes, I saw them come in on an Atakebune a couple of hours ago."

"I'm happy we're leaving tomorrow."

"So am I."

"Should we get everyone eating before we call it a night?" Saburo interrupted.

"Yes, sounds great." Kenji replied.

As if someone had rung a dinner bell, the kids came speeding down the ladder and took places around the new food that had been brought. Hanako and Riku started to hand out food to the children and they formed a circle in the center of the floor to begin filling up their hungry stomachs. The women continued to hand out food as the other members came down to eat, and they all formed a very familiar circle on the ground. Nami brought the lantern down and put it in the middle of everyone to take the place of the fire that usually lit up the group. Soon stories were being shared from members of the group, and Kenji saw more smiles from his friends than he had seen in awhile, and he could not help but smile himself. Saburo told a story of when he ran head first into the trunk of a tree when he was running from one of his friends during a game of tag and caused the children to erupt into fits of laughter. Even Aiko was struggling to keep her food in her mouth when listening to his story.

"And that wasn't even it!" Saburo continued. "After I ran into the tree my friend bumped into me and we both fell over!" This caused another burst of laughter from the group.

"Did you know I found another cave when I was younger that was different from the one we were in?" Riku began her own story.

"Where was it?" Jun asked intrigued.

"It was under my house!" Riku exclaimed. "And I found the craziest stuff inside..."

Everyone was now fixated on the new tale being told, and some people had even slowed their eating to listen. Kenji stood leaning on a pillar on the outside of their circle and watched happily as the stresses of the previous days seemed to have been lifted, if only for the evening.

"You've done really well keeping this group together and safe." Hanako said coming to join Kenji.

"We are almost free. I actually think it may work now."

"Of course it will work. We have you to thank for that."

"I didn't do this alone, we were thrown together and had to achieve this as a group."

"You're just being modest."

"Maybe, Ichiro said I should always focus on helping others before I focus too much on myself."

"He seemed like a wonderful man. I wish I had gotten to know him for longer." Hanako put a hand on Kenji's arm.

"He really was." Kenji replied taking a glance at the floor. "I have kind of an odd question for you." He said looking up again.

"What is it?"

"What's your mother's name? I have never actually known but we've been together so long I felt bad asking now."

"Yes, she is a bit more reserved than I am. Her name is Maru."

Kenji was taken by surprise and shot a look toward Hanako's mother who was laughing along with the rest of the group.

"What's wrong?" Hanako asked.

"Nothing, Maru is my mother's name. It just took me by surprise."

"Really? That's interesting. We're not related, are we?" Hanako laughed.

"No, I'm pretty sure we're not. Just a coincidence is all." Kenji grinned back.

"That's good because it would be strange to find out now."

"Definitely." Kenji agreed.

"Can I ask you a question?"

"Go ahead." Kenji was back to watching the group share stories.

"Why don't you talk about your father very often?"

"Since he wasn't around very often. He was trained as a Samurai and because of that, he wasn't allowed to have many material possessions or money. I'm not really sure if he was even supposed to have the type of family life he had with me and my mother."

"Was he there when Tokugawa went to Ikebe?"

"I think so, as long as he hadn't left again before they got there. I never saw him that day though."

"So, you don't know what happened to him?"

"My whole village went up in flames. If he didn't get caught in it then he would have been captured and surely committed seppuku." Kenji said with slight anger appearing in his voice.

"Oh." Hanako looked toward her friends not wanting to prod any farther.

"The only thing I have to remember him by is this." He motioned to the engraved sword on his back.

"It's nice to have something at least."

"Yes, I suppose."

"Kenji, Hanako! Stop sharing secrets and tell them to everyone!" Maku called jokingly.

"Oh, it's no big deal." Hanako stepped forward. "I was just reminding him about the time I beat him in an arm wrestle."

"What! Really?" Aiko laughed.

Hanako smirked and found a spot in the circle. Kenji shook his head and followed along.

"It wasn't even hard," she boasted.

Kenji shrugged and nodded giving Hanako her time in the spotlight with the children. Another laugh came from the children filling up the whole interior of the old warehouse.

As the last remaining children settled into their spots up on the second level, the building was filled with an almost ominous silence. Kenji placed one of the cloths over top of the lantern allowing only a few lines of light to creep through the sides so he could see where they were. The rest of the ground floor was illuminated by the full moon that shone high in the night sky through the second floor window. It gave off enough light that Kenji could patrol without the need to squint in order to see where he was going. The rest of the city had gone quiet and Kenji could only hear the waves ripple and crash into the side of the docks outside. He walked to the front entrance and took a quick look outside, reluctant to settle in to their new sleeping quarters. But to his relief, they were alone in this part of the city, and the old warehouse did seem to be a nice temporary gift from Aiko's friend. As he looked around Kenji could not get Aiko's friend's voice out of his head as if he had heard it once before. He brushed it off and started to think about their trip once more. He moved to Strider who had settled into a corner of the warehouse and lightly stomped his hooves as Kenji approached. Kenji held his arm out and let Strider rub his head into it before rubbing his neck. Kenji had created a bond with Strider, and knew he could not leave him behind. Strider was now coming along for the trip.

"Will you be happy on the island we find, I wonder?" Kenji asked as he patted the horse's shoulder.

Strider shook his head and stomped his hooves again this time with a little more force to the steps.

"What is it? Don't want to co-"

Suddenly Kenji's neck was wrapped up in an arm and he shot his hands up to pull down on the grip around his neck. The unknown assailant started pulling Kenji back and away toward the entrance. Kenji took his right leg and took a step back, hooking it behind the attacker's right leg before stepping up to be square with him and throwing his shoulder forward, causing the attacker to trip backward over his leg. The man recovered by rolling backward over his shoulder and standing up to face him, hands tightened to fists in front of his face. The man wore black clothing with a matching mask covering the lower half of his face. He looked to be unarmed but he appeared comfortable nonetheless. Kenji instinctively glanced up at his sleeping group and back toward the unknown man. He brought his hands up as the man rushed forward, shooting out two jabs, followed by a cross with his back hand. Kenji slipped his head to the right and then the left and followed with a parry at the man's cross punch with his right hand, before repositioning himself once more. Without giving Kenji time to recover fully the masked man shot out a right roundhouse kick at Kenji's ribs, which Kenji caught by his side, sliding away from it to lessen the impact. Without breaking his flow, the man switched his hips and leapt up, delivering another roundhouse kick with his free leg to Kenji's temple before landing back on his feet. Kenji tumbled sideways into the one of the pillars in the warehouse and a loud crack shot through the wooden beam. Immediately Maku shot up and looked down toward what was happening.

"Kenji!" He called out.

"Stay up there with them!" Kenji yelled back.

The attacker sprung forward throwing out a downward punch, which Kenji narrowly dodged, causing the man to connect with the pillar behind his head. Kenji slid back once more as the man spun around trying to connect with a spinning back fist to Kenji's face. Ignoring Kenji's order, Maku dropped down from the rafters to join in the fight. Maku lunged forward, striking out with a push kick, but the attacker caught his foot in front of his sternum and twisted his ankle, causing Maku to spin to the ground. Kenji followed up by closing the distance and shot out with a jab which connected with part of the man's jaw as he turned away. Kenji tried to take the advantage and got in close to throw a reverse elbow into the man's chest. Connecting with the elbow, the masked man stumbled backwards and lowered his stance. The whole gang was up now and watching from above with Naoko and Isas rushing down to help. As Naoko and Isas got to the ground floor Maku had gotten back up and was standing behind Kenji. The assailant eyed his targets and waited for the first move.

"Rush him!" Naoko yelled.

"No wait!" Kenji tried to caution, but it was too late.

Naoko moved first, running for the man's legs. He sidestepped him and shot a knee into his ribs sending him toppling to the ground. Maku and Isas moved together with Maku throwing a round house to the man's left side as Isas rushed him, readying a punch. The attacker caught Maku's kick and sent a counter kick to Maku's groin to which he bent forward in pain. Still holding onto Maku's leg, the man blocked Isas's punch hard out to the side and delivered a strong uppercut to his jaw, knocking him back into the wall. He threw Maku's leg to the side and Maku collapsed as Kenji came in with a jump kick aimed for the man's chin. The man stepped back but Kenji followed with a back kick, which forced the attacker to step to the side and follow with a push of his leg and a strong cross punch which hit Kenji's mouth. Dazed, Kenji tried to steady himself, but the attacker gave him a push kick to the chest and Kenji fell to the floor. Rolling to his side, Kenji swept his leg around and connected with the man's calf causing him to join Kenji on the ground. Kenji wrapped his legs around his opponent and pulled him in while sinking both his hands into his collar and around the neck. Pulling the man tight, Kenji turned his wrists in to tighten the choke. The man shoved his hand down and across Kenji's face turning his head to the side and forcing Kenji to let go. Kenji rolled back and brought his knee to his chest before releasing a kick to the man's nose causing him to stand and take a step back. Kenji stood up again and readied himself for more trying to control his breathing. The attacker wiped his nose under his mask which was now smeared with blood. He steadied himself before approaching Kenji with hands by his face once again. Kenji could see his opponent was losing energy and there was a good chance he would begin to fight desperately. Kenji waited for him to move closer and feinted forward drawing a punch from his opponent. Kenji responded by dodging his head and shifting his weight back and then forth delivering a jab that connected with the jaw. Before he even brought his hand back in, Kenji spun on the spot, leaned backwards and sent his foot flying into the side of the man's head. The man's neck jerked to the side and he fell into the nearby wall causing his neck to be pushed even more out of alignment upon contact. His body crumbled along the wall before slumping onto the floor and just like that, the moonlit fight had ended. Kenji rubbed his jaw trying to assess the pain he felt and looked back up at the group watching from above to ensure they were still alright.

"Ugh, what was that about?" Maku groaned while stretching his leg out to the side.

"Yes, who was that? Isas asked resting against the wall.

"He was a shinobi." Saburo answered from the rafters.

"A what?" Aiko asked concerned.

"An assassin. They are usually sent out for reconnaissance or espionage. Tokugawa must have sent him after us." Kenji said still trying to massage his jaw back to health.

"I thought their numbers were starting to thin out." Maku said.

"So, what happens now?" Hanako asked.

"All we can do is get some sleep. Tokugawa already knows we are here so he was probably only sent to gather more info or slow us down." Kenji said.

"We should make sure we are ready to move in the morning and get on the ship before his men arrive." Maku suggested.

"Get some rest for now. I'll deal with the body." Kenji said leaning down to pick up the corpse.

The group slowly made themselves comfortable once again and tried to get some rest for the remainder of the night while Kenji carried the body outside. He walked around the corner of the warehouse where some extra barrels and crates were stacked against the side wall. He dropped the body and shifted some crates off to the side to create an opening in the middle. Dragging the body into the newly created spot, Kenji then moved the crates back into place creating a small wall around the shinobi that would conceal him to anyone who was walking past. Satisfied with the placement of the corpse, Kenji made his way back inside and shut the door to the warehouse. When he climbed the ladder to join the others, he found they had already fallen asleep. Kenji found a corner and sat back against it. Leaning his head against the wall Kenji allowed his eyes to close for a moment and let his body relax. Kenji planned on opening his eyes back up to keep watch but his eyelids had different plans and before he realized it he was fast asleep just like the rest of his friends.

CHAPTER 21

~1590 - Ikebe Village~

"Do you have to go away again? You only just got back." Kenji pleaded.

"I'm sorry son, but you know I have my duties, I have to go but I'll come back before dinner time I promise." He bent down and gave Kenji a kiss on the top of his head.

"Father, before you go can I ask you something?"

"What is it?"

"I heard some of the adults talk about a word I haven't heard before, shinobi? What's that?"

He knelt down in front of Kenji and put a hand on his shoulder.

"The shinobi are bad people Kenji. They are spies and assassins and they fight without honour."

"But you fight with honour, right?"

"Of course. A samurai must always fight with honour and if he loses or gets captured, he always commits seppuku remember?"

"Yes father. I hope that never happens to you." Kenji said giving his father a tight hug.

"I'll be with you for a long time, but if that happens to me, I need you to understand that I must choose seppuku or else I can never see you again."

"Kenji it's time to go train!" Ichiro called out from the fields.

"Your mother and Ichiro will take good care of you and I'll be back soon alright?"

"I know. Be safe father."

"You too, son."

He gave Kenji one last pat on the head before turning and walking through the front entrance of Ikebe. Kenji watched his father until he went out of view before running off to join Ichiro in the fields. Ichiro was waiting with a pair of wooden training swords and as Kenji approached Ichiro smiled. He held out one of the wood swords and Kenji took hold backing up and preparing his stance.

"Alright, let's see if this time you get lucky and strike a fatal blow."

~1599 – Nagoya Warehouse~

Kenji woke up, blinded by a beam of light shining straight through the window and directly into his eyes. He held his hand up to cover his face as he stood and stretched out his arms before looking around at the others. To his surprise he seemed to be the last one to have gotten up. Everyone else was down on the ground floor packing what items they had into Strider's saddle or into the food crate and sacks Maku and Riku brought back the evening before. Hanako and Saburo were handing out some food that had been put aside for breakfast. Kenji walked to the ladder but stopped abruptly almost tripping over Aiko who had darted in front of him.

"Good morning sleepyhead!" Aiko giggled.

"Morning. I see everyone is almost ready to go."

"Yes, and while you were sleeping Saburo and I ran back to see my friend and he said the ship should be ready by the time we get there."

"Good job Aiko, thanks."

"You're welcome! I'm excited to show you around the ship later."

"I'm excited for you to show me." Kenji said trying to ignore the temptation to rub his eye.

"Kenji could I ask you something?"

"Of course, what is it?"

"Could you teach me how to fight like you do?"

"Why do you want to learn?" Kenji asked surprised by the request.

"Because it seems pretty dangerous now and I think it would help."

Kenji could not argue with her logic. The world had become drastically more dangerous since the war started and with Tokugawa now controlling Japan there was sure to be high tensions for the foreseeable future.

"I'll think about it. But how about we wait until we get everything packed away on the ship okay?"

"Okay! Thanks Kenji." Aiko beamed.

"Kenji!" Saburo had his hand raised and beckoned for Kenji to come over.

"Make sure you're ready to go. We'll leave soon." Kenji gave Aiko a playful punch on the shoulder before leaving to meet with Saburo.

"Did you sleep well?" Saburo asked as Kenji approached.

"It was fine. You should have gotten me up sooner though. I could have helped."

"You have done so much for us already and you needed the rest. But I have something I want to talk to you about."

Saburo turned slightly as if what he wanted to talk about was going to be overheard by others.

"I met with Aiko's friend this morning and there's something I think you should know."

"Is something wrong?" Kenji asked now concerned about what Saburo was thinking about.

"Kenji!" Again, Kenji heard his name being called and swivelled his head in response.

Maku came jogging toward the pair of them with a worried look on his face.

"Kenji there's something you should know."

"But Saburo was just-"

"It is fine it can wait." Saburo interrupted. "What is it Maku?"

"I overheard some of the guards talking in the market. They don't seem to know why but the city is getting a visit from some high-ranking soldiers today."

"They must be looking for us. Did they say who it was?" Saburo asked.

"It must be Tensu. Tokugawa would not bother with a personal visit." Kenji said.

"They expected them to arrive by the early afternoon so if we are quick, we should have time to get the ship stocked and set sail."

"Then that's what we'll do. Make sure everyone knows our urgency to leave."

"Will do." Maku set off again to spread the word and get everyone moving.

"So, what was it you wanted to talk about?" Kenji turned back to Saburo.

"It's okay, just a thought I had, but I'll let you get to helping everyone."

"Are you sure?"

"Yes, it's fine. We'll talk later." Saburo assured him.

Kenji turned again to survey the warehouse and see what still needed to be done. Most of the supplies had been packed away and Riku was busy brushing Strider, who was delighted by the pampering. Maku was holding the crate and Naoko was holding both sacks by his sides with everyone else ready and waiting by the entrance. Kenji moved to the front entrance and looked back at his group, who were looking optimistic now despite the new time crunch they were in. Perhaps the hope of their journey actually coming to an end kept their spirits up. By the end of the day they could be sailing far away from their home and off to make their lives somewhere better and safer for all of them. Kenji had to admit he was getting excited by the prospects and it felt like it was right at their fingertips.

"We're all ready to go?" Kenji addressed the group.

A collective nod was shared and the group left the enclosure of the warehouse and into the midmorning sun. Despite the sun being high in the sky it did not help it feel any warmer outside. The air was chilled with a brisk wind. Kenji resisted rubbing his hands together instead opting for his hands to be by his sides ready to raise them if any of the guards got suspicious. Even though they were so close to their goal Kenji could not help but be cautious. It was how Ichiro taught him to be, it was how he was raised. As the group approached the market, people were rushing to and fro, unbothered by the cooler weather and wanting their goods from the stalls. Some shop owners were covering their goods in sheets to try and protect them from the winds, only leaving a couple out to the side to showcase what they had to offer. When they entered the center of the market, Kenji took a glance at the stall owner whom he had threatened in defense of Jun. Walking past him Kenji noticed the man was rubbing his wrist almost instinctively as he passed but without looking up from his spot. He wondered if he had made the right call hurting him but decided he needed to focus on the current task at hand. It was easier for the group to get through the market area this time with fewer people rushing around today, likely because of the weather that had arrived seemingly overnight.

When they got closer to the edge of the docks, Kenji felt a tug on his shirt. He looked down to see Aiko pointing at something in the distance. Kenji looked up to see she was directing his attention to what must be her late father's ship. It was a fune of modest size and had a fairly thin deck in comparison to most ships docked around it – it had a single mast and sail protruding from the center of its deck. As the group began getting closer, Kenji could see the ship was steered by one main rudder hung from the back of the ship that had a large wooden handle attached so it could be steered from the deck. Toward the front end was a covered area just before the very front of the bow which almost resembled a small house. He could see the enclosed space had windows on the side which he assumed were reflected on the opposite side, and it looked spacious enough to hold Strider and the rest of the group. Kenji was surprised about the quality of the ship Aiko's father had owned, and he could not help but wonder how lucrative his career must have been to afford this type of ship. When they stepped onto the dock, a few wooden planks had already been placed down, creating a walkway from the dock to the deck of the ship. The party gathered around the handmade walkway before stepping foot on the ship.

"Please come aboard! Feel free to start storing your supplies!" A voice called out from the enclosed interior of the ship.

Aiko's friend was inside and Kenji could hear him working away on something which sounded like he was shifting things around. *Probably making sure there's enough room for us.* Kenji thought. He stood off to the side and motioned for the group to go on ahead of him to begin loading up the ship. Strider hesitated upon nearing the dock's edge and Kenji had to help calm him before he would cross with Riku. After Strider was on Kenji heard a gasp coming from the ship.

"Oh, I'm sorry! I didn't know you had a horse with you. Well, no problem there's room aboard." Aiko's friend said from where he was working.

Kenji could not help but grin to himself at the man's surprise but was also surprised himself by his attitude toward the whole situation. Kenji gestured for Aiko to come and join him back on the dock before she stepped out of eyesight. She skipped over to Kenji and stood on the ship in front of him.

"You are happy today, huh?" Kenji smiled again.

"I love ships, and being on the water, and sailing." Aiko said excitedly.

"I can see that. Do you mind if I ask about your friend?"

"No, do you want me to go get him?" She offered.

"No, it's alright I'll let him get the ship prepped for us. I was just surprised by how willing he is to go along with this. He must have been good friends with your family."

"Yes, he is. Mother said he came to live in the city around eight or nine years ago and my father and him really got along well."

"I'm glad he's being so helpful."

"Me too, I used to hear my father and him talk about things they did when they were younger and how they had to make up for them. So maybe that's what he's doing by helping us."

"It's certainly very nice of him."

"Excuse me, what's your business on the dock today?" A man spoke behind Kenji.

"We are just taking a family trip. All looked over and inspected don't worry." Kenji said as he turned around hoping what he said was actually true.

"Where is your destination?" The man prodded.

He was a tall man with a deep voice. He wore an old shirt with pants that were tattered and worn. Kenji took him for a dock worker, probably the man in charge of running things.

"I asked where you are going." The man asked again.

"Sorry yes, we are leaving for one of the islands off the coast. We have friends out there who own some land and we are going to stay with them a while," Kenji responded, hoping he did not have to expand any further.

"I'll have to get someone over here to inspect your ship and its occupants one last time before you depart."

"Of course, we'll be here." Kenji said with a smile.

The worker grunted and turned to leave toward the market.

"That's not good, I thought we have to leave right away?" Aiko asked.

"We do, we cannot wait around for an inspection. Go tell the others we need to leave soon and tell Maku I want to talk to him."

"Okay." Aiko went off to complete the task.

Kenji turned to keep track of the worker who was not heading in the direction he should be. Instead he passed through the market and walked off toward what looked like the road leading to the main gates. He followed him until he passed out of eyesight.

"What's going on Kenji?" Maku came up beside him.

"I was just talking to a dock worker who said he needed to inspect our ship before we leave. Except I think he's going to grab some of the guards instead."

"That's not good." Maku said stating the obvious.

"How close are we to being ready to leave?"

"Hopefully in the next couple of minutes. Everyone is just getting settled and storing our stuff away."

"Good, keep an eye out for anything that might be trouble for us. I'm going to stay here and see who that man comes back with."

Maku left to get back on the ship and Kenji began looking around to see if the movements of the citizens from the market had changed. Everyone seemed to be going about their day, so perhaps they did not know something was going on, or maybe they just did not care. Either way, the more unaware the population remained, the better off they were. After a couple of moments Kenji spotted the man he had talked to as he rushed around the corner and through the market. Following close behind him were four city guards all brandishing swords by their sides.

"Maku get back out here!" Kenji called keeping an eye on the approaching soldiers.

"What now?" Maku asked joining Kenji back on the dock.

"We have incoming. Are we ready to leave yet?"

"Almost, what do we do?"

"They definitely aren't coming for an inspection. We don't need to kill them just keep them away until we can leave."

"You said don't kill them? They already have their swords drawn!"

"I know but we aren't the bad ones here. We need the people to see we aren't trying to hurt them."

"Whatever you say boss."

The pair brought their fists up in preparation and waited until the men got closer.

"Ready?" Kenji asked.

"Ready."

The first one to arrive was the very enthusiastic dock worker who lunged for Kenji's abdomen, trying to knock him down. Kenji stepped to the side and, putting his hands on the man's shoulders, used his momentum to send him flying off the edge of the dock and into the water. A splash sprayed Kenji in the back as he turned to face the remaining threat. Maku was already ducking under the swing of one of the soldiers and he drove his fist into the next man's sternum, causing him to lose his breath and collapse to the wood. Kenji readied himself as the other two soldiers focused in on him. Stepping to his right out of the way of the first punch, Kenji put the man in between him and his other opponent. Once out of the way, Kenji blocked the punch with his forearm, keeping his hand open so he could grab the man's wrist and pull him into a roundhouse he shot into his stomach, causing him to collapse to the dock on his hands and knees. Kenji used the stunned man's body as a bench stepping onto his back and leaping forward throwing out a punch to the next man's jaw at just the right spot that twisted his neck and knocked him unconscious. Kenji landed and turned to face Maku who had closed the distance with the final soldier and lowered onto his knee to shoot an elbow into his groin to which he tumbled to the ground. The soldiers who remained conscious writhed around the dock groaning in pain.

"You fight dirty." Kenji grinned.

"You said not to kill them and they're not dead." Maku motioned to the men who lay at their feet.

"Fair enough."

"What is going on out here?" Hanako was standing at the edge of the ship.

"Nothing." They both shot back.

"That doesn't look like the nothing." Hanako nodded out toward more men who were coming through the market.

"Can we kill them?" Maku asked.

Kenji took a look at the approaching men and froze. Tensu was walking straight at them and perhaps even more threatening were the men who followed him. The two samurai Kenji had seen guarding the outside of Tokugawa's tent all that time ago were moving closely behind Tensu, their hands already by their waists, ready to grasp the hilts of their swords. The samurai brandished their battle armour and Tensu wore the same armour he had on when they attacked Sekigahara together.

"Maku go back on the ship and tell them we need to leave now." Kenji warned.

"I can help with them."

"No, I'll slow them down but we need to get the ship moving."

Maku had tried arguing before and knew the outcome. He sighed and obeyed what Kenji had said.

"Show off." He said stepping onto the ship.

As the threat drew closer, Kenji stepped out onto the stone path where the ground opened up as it transitioned into the market area. He reached back and pulled both swords from his back letting them hang down by his side. Tensu stopped a couple of feet in front of Kenji, and his two samurai positioned themselves slightly in front of him creating a small semi-circle in front of Kenji. Mirroring one another, the two samurai unsheathed their swords and stepped back into a fighting stance. Tensu stood with his arms crossed and his sword still hanging by his belt.

"I am under strict orders to bring you back to Lord Tokugawa." Tensu spoke in a loud firm tone making sure the surrounding civilians could hear him.

"I'm leaving here with my friends. We will not be a bother to anyone here."

"You and your friends will come with me."

"Tokugawa is a coward and a murderer and we will not live under a man like that." Kenji held his position and stared right back at Tensu.

"You will leave with me and my men NOW!" Tensu shouted. Kenji had clearly hit a nerve.

"I cannot let you take any more from us."

"So be it." Tensu took a deep breath in before exhaling and unsheathing his own sword, raising it up in front of him.

Kenji's eyes darted from one samurai to the other to see if they had made any subtle movements but they had stood perfectly still since readying themselves, as if they were on display. He raised his swords up and took a small step back preparing for the first strike to come. Tensu gave a nod and upon that signal, the two samurai rushed in unison toward Kenji. One strike came for Kenji's head while the other went for his stomach, and Kenji brought his right sword up to block while his other swung downward to parry away the lower strike. Upon contact, Kenji stepped back out of the way to keep his distance. The warriors repositioned themselves and came toward him again. This time Kenji sidestepped quickly to his left, trying to keep them in a straight line in front of him. If he only needed to fight one at a time at least then he had a chance. Before letting the one samurai come around his partner, Kenji struck out quickly, aiming for the warrior's collarbone. The samurai responded by blocking his strike and slashing back toward him. Kenji tried to turn his shoulder out of the way but he soon felt a searing heat in his left bicep. He could feel the warmth of his blood begin to seep down his arm but shook his shoulder in an attempt to ignore the feeling. The second samurai came around his partner now swinging his sword in an uppercut motion, and Kenji had to step back out of the way to avoid having the fight end right there.

Kenji heard Tensu let out a chuckle from his position behind his men and wondered how long it would take for him to come and join.

Kenji took a chance and went on the offensive, swinging up with both swords, forcing the samurai to move to their back foot. He used his momentum to swing downwards at one of the warriors causing him to bend to his knees and bring his sword up to absorb the hit. Moving in for support, the second soldier rushed Kenji, and Kenji swung backwards connecting with the incoming strike while keeping his sword locked with the other's sword. The standing soldier pushed hard against Kenji's block, forcing Kenji to lower his stance to keep his footing. Kenji twisted his wrist in an attempt to slash the standing warrior's wrist and he caused the samurai to back away long enough for him to focus in on his first target. The kneeling samurai let out a grunt while pushing back against Kenji, but Kenji had a free arm and turned his shoulder to drive his sword straight into the man's shoulder in between his shoulder pad and breast plate. The man cried out and Kenji drove a forceful knee into his chin causing him to topple to the ground. Turning now, he faced down the second samurai who was rushing back toward him. Kenji brought both his swords up in an 'x' over his head to block an incoming overhead strike from his opponent. Kenji bent low once more to keep his footing but suddenly shouted in pain as he felt steel cut his right calf. He stumbled slightly before regaining his footing once more and managed to keep his block up. The first samurai had swept his sword across Kenji's calf before returning to his feet. Kenji put all his weight forward allowing him to push back the overhead strike and shot out a back kick to the other samurai's chest with his uninjured leg. The man stumbled back as Kenji brought his arms over his head, and swung them back down with both connecting across his chest. The samurai collapsed in a pool of blood that began to stain the stone by Kenji's feet. This time Tensu rushed Kenji, but he drove his shoulder forward ramming into Kenji's abdomen. Kenji tried to bring his elbow up to strike down at Tensu but he was getting pushed back too fast. Instead Kenji opened up his left arm as Tensu wound up to stab at Kenji. Kenji barely got his arm out of the way in time but Tensu pulled back with his sword hard slicing into Kenji's side. Kenji curled over and dropped his father's sword from his right hand as he brought his arm up to put pressure on the wound. Tensu did not give Kenji time and had already wound his arm back for another strike. Kenji stumbled back and brought his sword up countering with just enough force to stop the strike from landing. Keeping his arm against his side Kenji stood as much as his body would allow and brought his sword up in front of him. Now the remaining samurai and Tensu moved as one both striking out at Kenji trying to cleave at his head. Kenji ducked to the right under Tensu's swing and repositioned himself behind his opponents.

Kenji tried to control his breathing but failed. He could feel every breath now and his body was struggling to stay up. Members of Kenji's group were standing at the edge of the ship now but Kenji could not make out who was who. Sweat had dripped down into his eyes and so he brought his arm up to wipe away what he could. As he regained clear vision, he watched as Tensu and the samurai once again ran toward him. His body was weak but his mind snapped into a place of focus as they approached. His turned his heel to feel a stone was beside his foot. Letting them draw closer Kenji stepped back slightly and pointed his toe toward the ground before flinging the stone up into the air. Tensu yelled as the stone connected with his nose causing him to stop his charge. For now, it was just Kenji and the samurai and Kenji brought his sword up to block the first strike. The samurai wound up again for another attack but Kenji struck out with a punch into his mouth. Stunned from the unexpected strike, the samurai stepped back and readied himself for what came next. Kenji wasted no time and swung up with his sword knocking his opponent's sword out of the way and creating an opening. Kenji brought his sword back the way it came and sliced right across the samurai's neck letting blood spray back into his face. The samurai collapsed to his knees before falling to the ground. Kenji looked onward to a furious Tensu who had wiped the blood from his nose down to his chin and was looking directly back at him. He saw the other sword he had dropped, behind Tensu, and was almost surprised Tensu had not grabbed it to use against him. Kenji took a breath in as far as his chest would allow before having to exhale from the pain in his side. As Tensu began walking toward him, Kenji could hear a voice inside his head. Kenji closed his eyes and shut his uncle out, not wanting to hear what he would think. Tensu went from a walk to run as he built his momentum up to strike out at Kenji. Kenji followed his lead and ran back toward him trying to compensate for his limp. As soon as Tensu got within range, he swung out to the side hoping to finish Kenji with a strike to the neck, but Kenji bent forward under his sword and sliced across Tensu's stomach as he ran past him. Tensu wobbled forward before falling to his knees behind Kenji. Kenji walked forward and bent down to pick up his father's sword from the ground and turned back toward Tensu, who was bent over his wound. Kenji shook his head continuing to block out his uncle as he walked up in front of Tensu. Tensu lifted his head to look up at Kenji with eyes that were not his own. They were terrified and pleading to Kenji without words as he sat on his knees in front of him. Kenji raised his swords up and crossed them over one another placing them down on Tensu's shoulders. Tensu began to breathe heavy before taking a deep breath in and closing his eyes.

"You have bested me." Tensu said as blood dripped from the side of his mouth.

Kenji started to breathe heavy now and he looked back toward the ship. He saw the faces of his friends staring back at him all with eyes wide except for Aiko who stared back at him as if they were having a conversation by the fire. Kenji stared back down at his beaten foe and tightened his grips of his swords.

"Ahhhh!"

Kenji pulled his swords sideways and felt the resistance of flesh and bone as he yanked his blades back. One single sound was heard when Tensu's skull cracked as it hit the stone. Kenji let his arms drop to his sides as he felt his body begin to give, and before he could take another step his world collapsed into darkness.

CHAPTER 22

Aiko watched from the deck of the ship as Kenji fell to the ground beside Tensu's body. She stood still as Maku and Naoko rushed out to where he lay and bent down to grab him. She watched as they carried him back to the ship and felt a hand grab her shoulder.

"Aiko it's time to go." Kazuo said.

She followed Kazuo across the deck of the ship and together they followed Maku and Naoko as they carried Kenji into the cabin of the ship. They placed him on one of the beds and Aiko stared as his hand fell over the side. Hanako rushed in after them just as Kazuo left to begin their departure.

"How is he?" Aiko asked almost in a hushed tone.

"He's hurt really bad and he's losing blood. Maku, grab me any cloths we have."

"On it."

"Aiko don't worry, I'll do everything I can but why don't you go make sure your friend is okay to handle the ship?"

"But I want to stay here." Aiko pleaded.

"Once I clean him up a bit I'll call you back, okay?"

A scowl crossed Aiko's face but she did as she was told and left to go see Kazuo. He was by the rudder of the ship and was busy calling out instructions to other members of the group. Some were letting down the sail while others were positioned on either side to make sure the sides were clear as they left port.

Once the sail was fully extended, the air latched onto it and the ship began to move. Aiko held onto the side as they pulled out of the docks and started making their way to open water. Once she steadied herself, she walked to the back of the ship to go see Kazuo.

"You okay Aiko? That was a lot back there." Kazuo asked while keeping his eyes fixed to the horizon.

"Yes, but I'm worried about Kenji."

"Well, he seems like a tough young man. I'm sure he'll pull through."

"So, I guess you're coming with us now?"

"I guess I am."

"Kazuo was it?" Saburo said as he walked out to meet them.

"Yes, what is it?"

"I believe I have something that belongs to you."

"Oh, and what is that?" Kazuo asked puzzled.

Saburo held out his hands and presented Kazuo with Kenji's engraved sword. Without saying a word Kazuo took the sword from Saburo and tightened his grip around it.

"I really never thought I'd see this sword again. It's been many years since I've held it."

"When do you plan on telling everyone?" Saburo asked.

Aiko's eyes grew wide as she realized what the exchange she just witnessed had meant.

"You're his father!" Aiko whispered.

"I haven't seen him in nine years and I had always feared the worst."

"Why didn't you look for him?" Aiko asked.

"I could not. I had to go far away after our village was attacked and I was captured."

"You didn't commit seppuku." Saburo stated.

Kazuo looked down at his feet before raising his head up again to speak.

"I saw an opportunity to escape and I took it. But it went against my code. By running away I had dishonoured myself and my family. Even if I knew that Kenji had lived, I could not have faced him after what I had done."

"Why didn't you tell me?" Aiko asked.

"Because after coming here I left all traces of my previous life behind. I needed to forget."

"You need to go see your son." Saburo said.

"I will. I need to get us to open waters first."

"You don't deserve to have that sword."

"You're right. That's why I gave it to Kenji's uncle to give to him."

"What will you do if he doesn't wake up?" Aiko asked in frustration.

"Once we hit open water, I will go see him."

"You need to go see him now!" Aiko yelled back as a tear rolled down her cheek.

"Aiko let's leave him, he clearly has an important job to do." Saburo said looking back at him.

Aiko spun around and walked toward the edge of the ship. She crossed her arms and put her chin down on top to look over the side and into the water. She watched as the water pushed up against the side of the ship and she looked hard to try and see her reflection in it. But all she could see was the rippling water the ship was cutting through as it moved onward. She loved the ocean and would always enjoy the times that she and her family went sailing, but none of those emotions were with her today. All she could think about was Kenji lying on that bed with his arm hung over the side and she began to cry. She tucked her head into her arms and cried about Kenji, about her home and about her mother and father who could not come with them on the ship. Pent up emotion was allowed to come pouring out for the first time and she cried until she struggled to breathe. She sniffled hard trying to stop the tears but she cried all the same;

until she heard Hanako calling her name. She lifted her head up and turned to look at Hanako who was looking back at her from the cabin's entrance. She was leaning against the doorway and was breathing heavy. Her hands and forearms were covered in blood but Aiko could not see the expression of her face from where she was.

"You should come see him," she called.

Aiko wiped her hand across her face trying to get rid of the remaining tears and ran up to join Hanako. As she approached the door her head was filled with emotions but the one that shone through the most was hope that she would get to talk to her friend again. She ran through the door almost skidding into the room and looked at the bed. The group was huddled around it but once she got there, they stepped aside to let her see and she let out a gasp but did not say a word.

"Hey kiddo, is it time for the tour?"

THE END

CPSIA information can be obtained
at www.ICGtesting.com
Printed in the USA
LVHW041628011120
670390LV00023B/645